THE DEADLANDS
SUMMER 2025

THE DEADLANDS

ISSUE 39, SUMMER 2025

© 2025 by Psychopomp. All Rights Reserved.

ISBN-13: 979-8-89116-016-3

psychopomp.com

Publisher: Sean Markey
Editor in Chief: E. Catherine Tobler
Poetry Editor: Nicasio Andres Reed
Social Media: Felicia Martínez
Art Director: inkshark
Nonfiction Editor: David Gilmore
Necromancer at Large: Amanda Downum
Copy Editor: Laura Blackwell
Copy Editor: Annika Barranti Klein
Designer: Christine M. Scott
Cover: *Garden of Shadow* by luseen

The Deadlands is distributed quarterly by:
    Psychopomp
    PO Box 36
    Woodbury, VT 05681

Subscriptions can be purchased at weightlessbooks.com. Individual issues can be obtained by joining our Patreon (with many deadly perks).
Join here: thedeadlands.com/patreon

SUMMER 2025

PSYCHOPOMP

TABLE OF CONTENTS

TABLE OF CONTENTS

THE CLOTHIER OF THE SUNLESS

Arda Mori

In this black-lanterned valley, only wraiths
blossom in lotus-white, bemoaning
their wind-shaped cloaks, which bind them
to the eternal ensemble of the bloodless.

My spinning wheel counts their footfalls
layering, then thinning into winter-dark roads.
Majesty, as you judge them, I sew their fates;
garments which name them in these sunless lands.

If you watch me still, pocket your wondering heart;
no amount of gauze can dress these bleeding heaps.
Mud-slow the spirits march, in sins of every color —
like powder, undone wishes pile upon my rooftop.

See the dead sovereigns, cape-torn and curse-chapped
wailing for the gold and crowns wasted on their temples.
Their hands, which gripped the throats of kingdoms,
rip each other's chests for tatters they once trod.

For those wilder than beasts, who you thrill to punish —
in the selves they once worshipped, they shall be adorned.
Yet though I twine their veins, scarf them with entrails,
I weep for the wounds which wet dawn's eyes, over and over.

Quiet are the strings ribboning my form, yet at times
one strums them into song, like you've once done —
like the beaten and guiltless, the sacrificed and small.
I leave them furs and winged shoes for their long walk.

Once my hearthrugs nursed laughter young and old;
familiar steps on the shadow road I await by my door.
Dyed in yellows of bonfires and letters, my palms
stretch like the silks and gold yarns I yearn to share.

Across millennia I've spun threads of sun and sea,
yet many times unclothed gusts have left me crumpled.
Secrets tenderly pressed or hatred like molten iron —
textures I shall remember, but can never recreate.

And if I must sleep forever, who shall veil me?
Not the ones I've robed, awash in flame or cloud.
Not the underworld's kings who have cast me down,
nor I, who desired more, and now dares not want.

Majesty, come — in your beggar's guise, so we stand free as before.
Above, the stars flower to summon both the dead and the living.
If I must sleep, I ask not for rose garlands or a diamond shroud,
only a little light to recall the sun of our days and all its tapestries.

Fiction

FOR THOSE WHO STAY BURIED

Amanda Cecelia Lang

CW: Domestic, physical, and emotional abuse

THE SIXTH or seventh time my husband buries me, I can tell by his jackknife grin that he thinks I'll finally stay down. My internal organs slosh, and he takes my feet for good measure and tosses them in the northern field for the wild things.

Worms in my hair, cubic zirconia rusting on my finger, voice box torn out somewhere along the way. I don't know what I need/desire/deserve anymore.

Not even when the three-legged fox returns my right foot to me, like a game of fetch.

———

I'm in the kitchen when he returns from the factory/the roadhouse/her place. The night sky beyond my gingham curtains hangs stony and outside of time, but fluorescent lights buzz over the yellow Formica table, and I've kept his porterhouse warm in the oven. Garlic powder and onion salt, special like he likes it.

Cursing/cringing/smirking at the flyblown sight of me, he relents into his chair, head of our table. I smile pleasantly with missing teeth and curtsey as I present his plate, the pearlbone knob of my left ankle smearing the linoleum. I used a byzantine cross stitch to secure my right foot, but he doesn't compliment the intricate needlework or fancy golden embroidery floss. I try not to let it worry me. Grateful just to have him home.

He hardly touches his meal.

———

I brush my gums before bedtime, spit all the ooze and messy feelings down the drain, preen for a kiss goodnight. Instead, he shrouds himself in bedsheets along the far cliffside of the mattress, like a man who might jump. He turns cold and rigid, plays dead. Am I oozing again?

There must be a surgery or a cosmetic that can fix me for him.

I know I'm not like other girls, not like the younger ones, or the older ones, or the ones in between. My uniqueness used to be what he adored/monitored/imagined about me. Not anymore. I'm not like her. Whoever she is. The specter in his eyes every time he turns away, goes away. So far faraway, until *I* become the specter buzzing around his weary head. Buzz-buzz little housefly, too loud in the ear, too irritating to the eye.

Sleep proves impossible without dreams, so I spill from bed and fold his socks and lick the black mold from the walls. I re-hang our old photographs. Over and over again, because when one goes up, another falls down, as if our years together never were. I refuse to believe he wills it. I peruse my empty closets and move over him while he snores, my ankle stump seeping into the floorboards.

There's a meat fork drying atop a dish rack in the kitchen, and I don't even fetch it. That's how I know we are real. Once, maybe twice, captured and vulnerable beneath the twitching eyelids of a dream, I think I hear him mumble/whimper/exalt my name.

Or perhaps that's just the wistful hum of blowflies.

———

He must have an early shift at the factory. He slinks through the shadow-bruised house with his flask and his steel-toed work boots in his hands. How sweet of him, not to want to wake me. Naturally, he finds me bushy-eyed and bright-tailed in the kitchen, nose freshly powdered and a griddle of eggs on the breakfast table. Yolks runny, an ooze of blood in the center, just how he likes them.

But this morning, he grumbles, says he doesn't have time for this crap. I nod and keep my insides in and stand by pleasantly as he slams out through the screen door, the dirt-clotted sky bleeding red with the dawn.

He forgot his sack lunch and his goodbye kiss. I'm delighted when he rushes back inside a few seconds later, passion/urgency/fury twisting his eyes, his toolbox rattling in his hand.

———

It's the three-legged fox who wakes me. Nipping my apron and my pelvic bone with quick needle-teeth, tugging me sideways from the shallow garden. Uprooted the daisy-roses, the untamed naughty thing. I sit up in a rain of thorny soil, gathering a bouquet of buds and stems and the splintered handle of a hammer. Mud chokes my right eye. I rub the side of my forehead, touch upon pulpy concave thoughts. The moonlight shines oddly upon me. Goodness, have I missed his supper? The fox whines, nips at me, tugging my apron strings, away, away.

But windows glow inside our slantwise marriage house, yellow and grimy, and I hear the record spinning, wobbly discordant jazz-time melodies. Two silhouettes swing-dance inside.

I didn't know we were expecting a guest?

I stand, torn. The fox bolts into the northern field, trailing ribbon-shreds of apron, her elongating shadow floating into the mudded sky on gloom and a phantom leg. And oh—

There are others gloaming in the field tonight.

How lovely. I see them rising, waiting, watching me with reflective silver eyes, toothless blackhole grins, inky anarchic curves and limbs, like gritty lines of wishes and watercolor bleeding into the wild barren nightscape. All of them slavering/lonely/ready.

———

I enter through the screen door and find a young woman sitting at my table.

Practically a baby doll in pearl earrings. Her sleepy eyes roll in sunshine sockets, lashes click-click-clicking as I approach the table, dragging my left ankle and a soiled smear of myself. She is as I was just last week/last year/last decade. Thin-poured waist, painted-plum lips, twiggy arms bent at the elbows. Her kisses have never tasted like mold.

Over the crackling, spinning swoon of jazz, I hear the shower running and wonder if he's scrubbing off her filth or mine. I smile, show her my tooth-hollows packed with dirt and severed roots. Our roots, *as in him and me,* squirming and tendril-deep.

The girl goes bloodless, demurs, compliments the cross-stitching around my right foot. But her fear of me and my envy of her make us sisters, for we are both wrong.

"It's cramped inside his ribcage," I tell her, but my jaw only clicks, and my words crumble out as loose dirt. I've forgotten my missing voice box.

"He doesn't want you," she babbles in a thousand other words. Gushes about him in all the ways that come freshly hatched, the yolk and blood of new lust/love/'til death, before everything starts to smear and run thin. Her shiny future with him pours from her, liquid as the organ-slurry inside me, and I wonder what vital parts she's already missing. When she pauses to take a breath, her face and breasts fold inward and melt into plastic obscurity, oozing onto the supper table and the bland grey meat she's prepared for him.

She forgot the garlic powder and onion salt, I think smugly.

The shower creaks to silence, and when he steps out, slick and whole in his towel, us girls sit up straighter, shed our snakeskin sisterhood. She scoops herself together, resolidifying, bones and bits knitting into new and exotic shapes, all for him. Survival of the pertest.

Glaring/sneering/true-heart-beating at me, his handsome grin spreads like yellow grease, and he opens lewd arms. To her.

She hurries over on tiptoe doll-feet and offers him the meat fork.

———————

The three-legged fox makes a great leaping game of returning me to myself. Though, somewhere in the muddy northern field, my long-missing voice box begs her not to. There's not much left of me. A breast here, an ankle there, the lower hinge of my jaw.

The fox fetches other pieces, shards of puzzles that shouldn't belong, but oddly do. A pearl-earring ear that isn't mine, false ribs and floating ribs, a sleepy eye, a tiptoe doll's foot. A few scraps of me, a few scraps of someone on the side. I wonder how many hours/days/prayers she lasted. Before the reek of my festering memories clung to her, before her nagging kisses fatigued him. *We give so much, don't we?* I ask no one and everyone in particular. I miss the scratching of my heart, the pesty, hope-stained wild thing gnawing at its cage.

The silhouettes from the field gather around my incompleteness with warped black-velvet curves and patient quicksilver eyes. The fox whines and hop-scratches at the mud, unearthing thorns and twigs, splintery picture frames and rusty meat forks, wire birdcages and cracked porcelain ruins. Gathers anything she can to fill my dotted lines and gossamer hollows.

Odd how the love of a small thing can be a big thing.

I teeter over my husband on rib-bone legs while he sleeps. Wondering, wondering.

How he can be so content/shameless/intact when I am in pieces?

Stale kisses molder where once I bloomed a voice. The backwards-slanting earth and silver-eyed shades of the field flicker past our naked bedroom windows.

"Do you see yourself?" I hiss at him, every word shredding inside my rusty cheese-grater throat. What does his consummate wholeness say about my worth? Savage indifference picks away at the soul. But whose soul?

Who is this void I keep chasing?

The three-legged fox springs onto the bed, sniffing, baring needle-bone teeth.

My husband's eyes crack open along serrated edges. He glares past the fox, sees only the remaining bits of me standing here, jawbone/ankle bone/jeopardy. At once, his hands hook into fists and he lashes out at me, tries to bolt upright.

The fox pounces playfully, places a single paw upon his chest, pins him down. Phantom paw or flesh-and-blood paw, I'm not sure which she uses. Every creature is stitched of both.

My husband's muscles and bones lock up rigid. He falls paralyzed, mouth gaping like an empty grave as he curses me with vile names that aren't my own. *Nag/drag/hag!* I lean over him, and the door of my birdcage-ribcage swings open. Hard-packed dirt crumbles from my unhinged jawbone into his open mouth, turning to mud upon his greasy tongue, inside his swampy throat.

My toothless cavities ache and needle and squirm. Our roots, *his* and *mine,* push up through my gums and snap loose, falling into his mouth, reseeding him. My single sleepy doll-eye rains nourishing tears.

And how dare I share myself with him! His furious screams become an open garden. Green buds sprout from his blackest soils, and slow curls of lacy vines escape his teeth and tangle upward, entwining the weeds and worms of my hair.

He fights this new growth, naturally he does. He thrashes against the fox's paw and the indignity of his paralysis. He tries to snap teeth like futile hedge clippers. But these vines are too sturdy, the beanstalks too wished-upon, born of all the diamond-ring promises he sowed, born of all the once-upon-a-times and happily-ever-afters he refused to nurture.

Even now, I wonder, wonder... What is happiness to this man?

What is it I need/desire/deserve from him?

He begins to choke. The shimmering wild-growth from my inner field is too much for him. Retching, eyes bulging. Poor put-upon thing. I tilt my earthen head.

Wind and grave shadows glisten beyond our window, and the moonlight sharpens, curve of a scythe. I extend my makeshift bones, my meat-fork hands, and pluck stems and vines from him, culling weeds. With our final roots tossed aside and withering on the marriage bed, he sucks in vital new breath. He actually looks relieved/self-gratified/aroused. I don't stop there.

Surely this man has *something* to fill my broken spaces. I thrust my rusty sharp arm down the pit of his throat. I burrow elbow-deep, chest-deep, through his muscle and rancor, until my fork-twine fingers stab the invisible organ throbbing inside.

I yank it free with a spray of black blood. It spasms once, twice, then melts to tar in the moonlight, oozing all over the floorboards.

The fox tilts her head at me and whines, as if to say, *well now, that's less than useful.*

I return to my husband, who never needed a heart to survive. He watches me with glinting, undying contempt and a bloody, entitled mouth. I'm not what he wished for either, but we knew that already.

Sometimes a wife's gotta dig deeper.

Nothing remains inside his chest cavity, so I dissect the rest of him, repurpose him, arms and legs first, like pulling petal-wings off a fly, like casting out one last wild daisy wish.

He loves me not.

For our happily-ever-after, I turn him inside out, muscle by muscle, bone by bone, until his wholeness becomes nothing but sagging meat and void. I had hoped to plug his pieces into my missing gaps, a pelvic bone here, a foot there, lots of sacred ribs.

But everything from him comes twisted and toxic and over-inflated. Nothing fits properly, nothing he has can puzzle me together again. Not even when I reach his festering soul-center, a cavity oozing a single maggot root.

The fox growls, low in the throat and full of thorns.

I straighten my rose-branch spine, and my sleepy doll-eye flutters open all the way. From the knotted intestine of the man, a stagnant reek/purpose/spirit rises into the bedroom, just barely. Before I can clasp it in meat-fork hands, it flits and fizzes away in a hiss of noxious steam no bigger than a blowfly.

There are no prayers after that, not for him.

His discarded chunks and the black tar of his heart drip around the bedroom something foul. The whole house is a muddy sight in need of a mop, and the breakfast eggs need fixing in between all that. I grab a sponge and fill a bucket with soapy water from the kitchen sink.

But the three-legged fox whines and scratches at the screen door, wind-touched and eager to be free of old routines. These routines that held me together for so long—but only for so long. I drop the bucket where I stand, swipe the eggs off the counter as I pass them by. Crack, crack, yolks and blood.

With each step I crack, too.

My jawbone loosens, my breast sags, my ankle knob twists, and I crumble, crumble, crumble. Pieces falling away, shell to ephemeral dust, shedding this makeshift cocoon until my rummaged bones slump and I collapse upon the three-legged fox, pounding with flesh-and-blood heartbeats, phantom heartbeats.

As we exit through the screen door, only she holds me up.

But I'm not alone out here.

The silver-eyed shades from the northern field and the jagged-vast world beyond are waiting. They surround me in a tangled Godspeed gloom, a hoary resilience, and a crooked crown of hard-won spring blossoms. Once cast aside, once buried, an inner wilderness dug them free. Their crooked bones melt into mine, and mine into theirs. Hardening, we reinforce each other, our battered heartbeats weaving an elaborate arterial stitchwork. Together, vast yet singular, we become something different, something myriad.

Something released/empowered/dangerous.

We need only ourselves, our wild animal selves.

Racing through the feral grasses, wind kissing our hair and fur and scars, our throats shriek and shimmer and shake the night. Above us, the moonlight cuts a beautiful hello through grave-soil clouds. Behind us, the slantwise marriage house fades into the night, a stain upon the darkness.

And I don't look back/I don't look back/I don't look back.

QUERY TELLING ON OTHER ELDER

Michael Hessel-Mial

By Cadmium Lattice, as told to Mended Relic, ca. 12,000,000 hours past

ADDRESS: records/non-operations/narrative_set/just/cadmium_lattice/-2*1/REF

PARSING CREATOR ABSTRACT:

_I_Tran_Scribed_This_Sad_Sto_Ry_Of
_An_Ast_Er_Oid_Dwel_Ler_Fran_Tic
_Ly_See_King_Her_Kin_When_The_Sta
_Tions_En_Ded_…_As_The_Hac_Ker
_Sto_Ry_Tel_Ler_Re_Ports_They_Could
_Not_Help_Her_But_We LIMIT REACHED

ENTRY:

Band!
A dweller comes looking for her other elder,
Because he has been separated from her.
A hacker helps by querying Frostlake,
But Frostlake is dying and can't compute any more.
The dweller goes home without finding him.

I only got this from someone who passed it along:
After the deathless ones would split the asteroids,
Dwellers would come looking for their relatives,
And hackers would use planetseeds to help.
It wasn't allowed for hackers to do this,
But hackers would send packet-query pulses to the planetseeds to help.

I only got this from someone who passed it along.

Well!
I have this query recorded:
"I'm looking for someone who's been separated from me;
He has four names but I can't find him"—
"Give me the genetic signature"—
"We don't share a genetic signature"—
"Give me the names of your conductor, director, and crèche"—
"He isn't my conductor, director, or crèche"—
"Tell me why you're looking for this person"—
"I'm going to have my pairing and I need my other elder"—
"Tell me about who this person is"—
"When I was one hundred twenty-five thousand hours,
My crèche and my conductor didn't like my girlfriend;
We were both becoming directors,
And my relations didn't want two directors together.
I flew away and a man found me.
His name is Understory Shoal Troposphere Counterfloat.
He told me, You know by my name that you'll be safe with me.
He became my other elder and helped me feel safe.
I came back to my relations feeling safe.
Then the sectioning happened and I couldn't find him.
I'm about to pair with my girlfriend and I need my other elder"—
"Tell me the query and I'll transmit it to the planetseed"—
"Ask the records about his name and placement gatherings"—
The hacker transmitted the query and dataset bundle;
They pulsed it into the atmosphere of the planetseed.
The query retrieved no record sets.
The dweller submitted another query:
"Ask the records about his name and puberty gatherings"—
The hacker transmitted the query and dataset bundle;
They pulsed it into the atmosphere of the planetseed.

Well!
I have these record sets memorized.
I have three extant records,

And none of them match.
Retrieving first record set:

"I call to Counterfloat Canopy Sandbar Exosphere

Oil the aperture and keep it partly open

The iron opens out, the titanium stays locked away forever

The craft trembles, ready to launch."—

Retrieving second record set:

"I call to Shoal Midstory Ionosphere Crossfloat

Oil the aperture and do not close it

The iron opens forward, the titanium draws inward"—

Retrieving third record set:

"Listen! Understory Channel Mesosphere Forefloat

You're asked to prepare the aperture,

So that nobody leaves it open or closed,

Because the craft is trembling, ready to launch,

And you are not yet ready."—

The dweller was unhappy to not find her other elder.

The hacker told her that Frostlake was dying.

The dweller submitted another query:

"Ask the records about his name and pairing gatherings"—

The hacker transmitted the query and dataset bundle;

They pulsed it into the atmosphere of the planetseed.

Well!
I have this record set memorized.
I have one extant record,
And it does not match.
Retrieving the record set:

"Listen! Forefloat Exosphere Watershed Midstory

Listen! Troposphere Mouth Canopy Counterfloat

Your mouth is full of ice, full of grit,

You cannot ask me to pair you yet,

Because I'm going to sleep.

Wake me up!"—

The dweller was unhappy to not find her other elder.

The hacker told her that Frostlake was dying.

The dweller submitted another query:

"Ask the records about his name and placement gatherings"—
The hacker transmitted the query and dataset bundle;
They pulsed it into the atmosphere of the planetseed.

I only got this from someone who passed it along:
The asteroid dwellers were bad at building crèches.
The hackers were still learning to build crèches,
But they did not have other elders.
Hackers and dwellers would pair director and director;
They would pair conductor and conductor.
I only got this from someone who passed it along.

Well!
I have these record sets memorized.
I have two extant records,
And neither of them match.
Retrieving first record set:
 "Who has the infants? Rinse them! Rinse them!
 Who has the infants! Rinse them! Rinse them!
 Who will choose the lots for us? Pull them! Pull them!
 Who will choose the lots for us? Pull them! Pull them!
 It's time, my friend, Thermosphere Shoal Understory Rearfloat"—
Retrieving second record set:
 "It's time my friend, Channel Midstory Forefloat Exosphere,
 Rinse the infants, pull the lots!
 Rinse the infants, pull the lots!
 Your home is streaked with silicates;
 It is time to relocate"—
The dweller was unhappy to not find her other elder.
The hacker told her that Frostlake was dying.
The dweller submitted another query:
"Ask the records about his name and preparation gatherings"—
The hacker transmitted the query and dataset bundle;
They pulsed it into the atmosphere of the planetseed.

Well!
The query returned no record sets.
The hacker explained that Frostlake had died;

The hacker explained that the planetseed had died.
The planetseed's atmosphere had died,
And it could not return record sets.
The hacker offered to search starborn record sets,
But the dweller refused.
The dweller didn't want to search starborn record sets.
She didn't know if her other elder had died,
So she waited for three cycles.
Then she went home.
Her query did not find the other elder for her pairing.
Band!

USER-ADDED RECORD:
Along with being a flawlessly preserved example of the "query telling" performance genre once beloved in the first generations of hackers, this entry represents a unique historical moment. The poem reveals how the collapse of the Frostlake planetseed impacted the dweller population of system Wildcat. Between eras dominated by a station economy and by a sublight economy, dwellers would approach hackers with illicit requests for data retrieval, often to help locate lost loved ones. Though we cannot determine this dweller's specific kin type, we recognize her grief at the death of Frostlake and at her failed search. However, the most significant value of this entry is its documenting of many traditions that are kept fiercely secret by asteroid dwellers. Now, other readers may benefit from these words, even in their limited and fragmentary form. Conductor of the Records, Strong Era.

Fiction

EVERLASTING

Daniel Oluremi

EVEN HERE, the hospital sounds bounce off the dense air around me. They ripple away and towards me in the blue light. The distance between me and my still, supine body grows, subtly so, with each passing moment.

I will never like this place. There are many things about it that I have forgotten over the years and ends. The air is frigid, and my heart beats weakly, slowly. I still breathe. The cold inches up my body, beginning at my feet and fingertips. Still, here, I remember what completeness feels like. Ordinary and full, like clean air moving through young lungs. My knees are not weak, my back does not ache. I stand strong for the first time in many years. My head is not cloudy, and my vision is not hazy. Importantly, my cancer will die with me, now—both of us lost in the end.

Moments before Death comes for me, I contemplate my body like a stranger. I feel a sloppy mixture of numbness and self-pity. My gaunt frame sinks deeper into the hospital bed. Jide sits by my side, his hand brushing my hair as he smiles and whispers to my body. I cannot hear him, here, but he knows. He also knows I am not coming back this time. His last words to me as I slipped into this place were a prayer.

"May God strengthen me to bear what remains of me till we meet again, my love." My heart broke at the tremble in his voice. In my pain, I could only hum and smile, squeezing his large hand until I couldn't anymore.

Ọlájídé. The tones in his name are my only warmth now, in this place. I smile and imagine him smiling in return. I hope to never forget the song his name has sung in my heart all these years. I hope to find him in Everlasting, though not anytime soon. At sixty-five years of age, three years older than I am, Jide is very much healthy. *I hope he doesn't forget me, too,* the sour thought tightens my chest. My forearms and legs begin to itch from the cold as I blink and turn away from my body and my love. They grow colder when I see her.

———

In more ways than one, Death looks like my mother. She is clad in a dark buba, with a long wrapper tied tightly over her chest. Her plaited, greying hair is loosely bound in a scarf cut from the same material as her clothes. Like màámi, Death is plump and short, and astonishingly beautiful—age barely bridles her waxy mahogany skin. Her lips are black and full. I could bet that if she parted them, I would see a gap in her teeth.

Unlike màámi, whose eyes were milk and honey, Death's eyes are jet-black, and they bleed thick blood down her cheeks. A string of stormy clouds sits on her head like a crown, journeying slowly around her. As Death takes small steps towards me, color drains from the surrounding world, escaping away to the edges of my vision like a drop of dye in water. Unlike màámi when she was alive, Death never speaks to me. Not now, not in all the six times I have come here before.

Of course, my mother would have hated such a comparison. No one I know despises Death as much as màámi did. In fact, before she died, màámi warned me against organizing any burial rites for her. She wanted no prayers or sentiment. She intended to go complete and rebellious into Everlasting. I remember her red, teary eyes those many years ago. I felt her anger and fear as she drew deep breaths, then shallow breaths, and then no breath. But her contempt for Death was not without cause.

For most of her life, my mother mourned one child or the other. She gave birth to six àbíkú children before me—stillbirths, miscarriages, or sick children who never spent up to a year in her arms. Her first child died on the day of its naming ceremony, passing quietly in her room while people pounded yam and served rice in the tents outside. My father told me that my mother's scream swallowed the soft band music whole. He said she screamed until she passed out. The other children signaled their departure with rippling pain in her womb, butchering hope within her again and again. Leaving trails and blotches of punishment for her incredulity.

So when màámi saw that I lived past the one-year mark, when she realized with those calculating eyes of hers that I wasn't going to die on her like the others, she took me to her brother, an herbalist of great acclaim in our village.

In those weeks of fasting and bathing in concoctions, they performed a grounding ritual to tether me to life. With blades, spices, and incantations, they inscribed six small marks on the back of my neck. One every three days. One for each of the siblings I should have had. One for every sliver of my mother's heart that Death had carved off. Each incision was a promise, a deterrent. A reminder to Death, the Child Stealer, that she had done enough already. I would be spared six times, without contest. A year before then, at my naming ceremony, my father had named me Janet. After that ritual, my mother only ever called me Ẹniọlọ́runòpa—the One Who God Would Not Kill—or Eni, for short.

––––––––

Now, as Death nears me, I remember the last time I saw her. Suddenly, strength leaves me, dragging away my peace with it. In their place is the inexplicable darkness of loss. The totality of hurt that blinds and bleaches the future of any vibrancy. I realize, now, that this darkness never really left me all these years. It just shrunk and hid somewhere in me. Only fleeting happiness or the other distractions of life held it back, like a reddening towel over a bleeding artery.

From the first end, during a ghastly accident, till the fifth one, when my troop was ambushed while on active duty in the army during the Biafran War, I enjoyed my gift. But I died the sixth time from stupidity and eclampsia. I imagine that if she had been alive then, màámi would have watched me with pain and anger as I gasped for breath that day. As I seized until I stilled. Now, I almost laugh at my stubbornness. Why did I think I could bear children when my own mother had failed? Why did I try? In a hospital bed like the one my dying body now lies in, I pushed my daughter from my womb, manic from understanding the ramifications of failure, until we both came to this terrible place.

I still remember the insanity. The itching and trembling that raked through me when I saw Death cradling my dying daughter in her arms. When Death got to hold her, even though I never would.

I rushed towards Death, who gently dabbed my daughter's wet head with a corner of her wrapper. She eyed me defensively. I shook my head vigorously as a sense of future grief threatened to destroy me.

"No, she will not die. She *cannot*." I felt a sharp pain at the back of my neck as the sixth incision burned off. Surely my gift would work for my daughter.

But Death watched me silently as I unraveled. I shouted into her silence. "Spare her, too! Please!"

But Death shook her head. I fell to my knees, my failing heart thudding.

"Please take me instead then! Surely you want me more than you want a child!"

Her eyes scanned me, but then she sighed. That was not part of the deal. So she turned away.

"Come back here! Oh, so you will take her too, *Child Stealer!*" I screamed with vitriol, before bursting to laughter at the joke that life had made at my expense. "What world am I supposed to return to? What future of mine can have meaning now?"

And in that agony, Death left me cold and colorless.

I am still cold, and everything is beginning to blur now. Death waits a few feet from me. The pain of my loss is now like the healed stub of an amputated limb. It feels far away, and so it seems inconsequential that I should hold a grudge after all these years. I want to hate, but hate doesn't want me.

As usual, Death rests a small basket of fruits on her left hip. The fruit selection is uncanny. I see a bunch of bananas, a split coconut, a couple of cashews, three papayas, and one cherry mango. In the many times I have almost died, there were always differences in the number and type of fruits in the basket, but there is always one mango. The mango Death always extended to me and I always refused.

Now, with all my incisions spent, I cannot but reach for the fruit. It is ripe but firm, with a spray of cold water on it, and it feels just as real as I am.

When I bite into it, my eyebrows perk up. The juice floods my mouth, agitating senses I didn't know I could feel. My lips quirk into a tight smile. Who would have thought the end would taste so sweet? That the suffering and toil of our short time on earth was punctuated with delight? Death watches me as I chew. As usual, her eyes bear no grudge or sympathy. Around us, lines and dimensions warp, instinctively mixing together like watercolor. Though we appear to remain still, we have moved many feet from my corner in the hospital.

When Death turns and begins to walk away, I know to follow her. As I take those steps with her, I think about my encounters with the woman with the fruit basket at the beginning of the end. The silent understanding between us every time I refused her. Our shared confusion and contention. My anger and her indifference. Then the reality of what is to come cuts through my pain and fear, revealing a lone truth in the dark. *I will miss her.* Emotion floods my dying heart, and then I do something I never thought I could. I cover the distance between us and reach for Death's free arm.

I hold my breath as Death spins. The hospital sounds mute. There is shock on her face, but she still doesn't speak. She remains strong in spite of my intrusion. Color drains away from where I am joined to her. In this moment, she feels like me in a way I cannot describe. I let out my held breath.

"I am grateful, Mother," I say as I gently squeeze Death's arm. This place ripples in synchrony with the fickle dredge-beats of my heart. It moves as if it gasps. "I have never taken it for granted."

Color pours back around us, capturing the sparkle in Death's dark eyes. I nod, answering the hidden question in those eyes. Even now, in the end, I acknowledge that though I have suffered, I have enjoyed what only very few people ever did. Many chances at life. Many escapes from the end. In my tragedies, I realize that I have had plenty worth losing. And I won in love with Ọlájídé, who I would not have met if I had never stood up from that accident at nineteen.

We wait in the silence for a brief moment. My hand slowly falls from her arm, though my eyes remain fixed on hers. When Death recovers, she nods, too. A softness falls on her face before she points behind her. I look in the direction she is pointing and I see a small dot of light in the distance, charging towards us like a train. It expands as it nears us, consuming everything in its path.

Everlasting. It is time.

I turn to see it all for the last time. The hospital sounds are back. I see the doctor has come to pronounce me dead. Jide's head is bowed, his body shakes from crying. *I am sorry, my love,* I think as my heart stops. When I turn to my side, Death is now a little boy with black eyes and blood tears, and a revolving crown of stormy clouds, headed away, towards a man convulsing at another end of the hospital ward. The basket of fruits awkwardly sits on his small head.

As I turn back to Everlasting, which is now larger than life, I know that everything else is in the past. I grin, a strange youthful excitement surging through me. I have lived! Now I have died! I am grateful. The cold will end soon.

As Everlasting collides with me, I feel it. In a moment, I know it in a way only the dead can.

Bright light in warm light. Perpetual. Forevermore.

BLIND DATE WITH A CORPSE

RJ Aurand

IT'S A WARM late spring evening. I'm wearing a blue sundress patterned with flowers and doves. My legs are freshly shaved, and my lips are painted a shade that's much too bright for my complexion. I squint against the golden hour sun as it gleams through the van's windshield and push up my glasses as they begin to slide down my nose. My boyfriend, Alan, is driving. We're on a date—a rare occasion, since I live on the other side of the state and only get to see him every six weeks or so.

There's also a dead body in the back seat.

In the little mountain town where I grew up, two family-owned funeral parlors serve the majority of residents in the area. When someone passes away at home of natural causes, one of their hearses will inevitably turn up a few hours later to collect the body. I have childhood memories of watching through my great-grandmother's windows as a pair of men in black suits wheeled her neighbor out on a white-sheeted stretcher and loaded her into their hearse.

It doesn't work like that everywhere, though. Alan lives in a busier part of the state, where seven cities meld together into a major metropolitan area that boasts several hospitals, dozens of funeral homes, and a much higher rate of homicides and traffic fatalities. The funeral homes here don't have the resources to send out a crew every time they need to retrieve a new client. Nor does the medical examiner's office, which has its hands full autopsying the bodies it already has on-site. Instead, they employ a private contractor to collect bodies from hospitals, homes, and crime scenes—a removal service. Alan is one of their drivers.

Corpse removal is the kind of profession that typically prompts a double take from people when they ask what you do for a living, followed by an incredulous *Why?* The answer, in Alan's case, is that he wants to be a mortician, and this line of work seemed like a good way to gain experience until he can find an apprenticeship. At his company, things work like this: (1) he's on call 24/7, rain or shine; (2) he needs to respond to death calls in an hour or less; and (3) because of that constraint, any time he leaves the house he dresses in his funeral suit and drives the corpse wagon—a standard minivan modified to accommodate two stretchers in the back—so he can head out at a moment's notice. The amount of work he does in a given day depends on how many people die. Sometimes I visit and he only goes on one call the whole weekend. Others, I barely see him at all. It's macabre, but it becomes normal faster than you'd think. With that being said, I still have a fight-or-flight response to hearing the iPhone's *Church Bells* alarm, having been startled out of my sleep by a death call on so many occasions.

This inevitably leads to some quirks. One of those is that any time we go to a sit-down restaurant, Alan asks for the check as soon as we order so we can leave right away if we need to. This practice usually confuses the wait staff, but it is efficient—even if it means I never get to order dessert. Tonight, I'm halfway through my salad when a call comes in, and I wince at him with my fork poised halfway between my plate and my mouth.

"It's pretty close this time," he says after he hangs up and plugs the address into his phone. "Want to ride along?"

The first of my great-grandfathers died when I was six. That was my earliest experience with human death, and I remember listening in as kids do while my parents dithered over whether or not to allow me to attend his visitation. He was being cremated, so his body wasn't going to be made up the same way an embalmed one would be. They were worried that I would be frightened of him without the glasses and dentures and hearing aids I was accustomed to seeing him wear. Ultimately, they decided to bring me along. My memories of that hour are deeply shadowed. I can picture him on the dais, unadorned but recognizable. He remained my great-grandfather, only still and quiet.

Things had changed by the time my great-grandmother passed away five years later. She had been embalmed, and at some point during the intervening years, I had acquired the notion that I was supposed to be terrified of dead people. Indeed, as other mourners were seated for the service, my sister and I worked ourselves into hysterics at the thought of going near the open casket. I loved my great-grandmother, but I didn't want to look at her. I especially didn't want to touch her. From the far end of the chapel, I was convinced that I could see her breathing. In the end, my mother had to ask the funeral home staff to lead us to our seats via a different entrance so we wouldn't have to walk past her while the lid was open.

"If you hold their hand, it's like touching a table," I remember her trying to explain to me later. "They're not in there anymore. It's not scary, and it doesn't have to be sad, either. A body's just a thing."

I ride along with Alan, mostly because I don't want to seem uncool, and partly because I'm studying to be a nurse. I know that I'm going to encounter my fair share of dead people in the future. We park outside an unassuming brick house on a quiet street. He pulls a stretcher out of the back of the van, and I fiddle with my phone in the passenger seat while I wait. Ten minutes later, he returns with a shrouded body and loads it into the vehicle. I eye it warily in the rearview mirror. It isn't moving. Its nose and knees make little peaks in the sheet. I can't smell anything weird yet.

He starts the van, and we head for the family's preferred funeral home.

Church Bells.

He looks at me apologetically. "This one's further out."

I shrug, although my skin is crawling, and we make a U-turn into heavy traffic.

———

The NICU I worked in after graduating from nursing school had an exceptionally high mortality rate. There were several reasons for this, but the biggest contributing factor was that we were the highest level of care in the region, which meant that the patients we admitted were frequently born to mothers from our high-risk obstetrics program, fell just shy of the hazy line we refer to as the "point of viability," or had already significantly deteriorated at an outlying facility before being transferred to us for end-of-life care. It wasn't uncommon for our unit to witness a dozen deaths in a week.

Death in the NICU is never a happy occasion. No one checks in to the hospital to welcome their baby expecting to go home with empty arms. Even a standard NICU admission is typically a chaotic, unplanned, and traumatic experience for parents, whether it's their first child or their eighth. "I could never do what you do," nurses from other units frequently said when we crossed paths. "It's too sad." Funnily enough, I felt the same way about their specialties.

At the height of the COVID-19 pandemic, when our hospital was feeling the strain of the nursing shortage and an unprecedented surge in patients, our leadership began floating pediatric nurses to adult floors as "helping hands" for the staff there. On one occasion I was sent to the trauma ICU, where I shadowed a nurse named Madeline, dual-signing on medications and assisting with patient care. Although we had been nurses for the same length of time, I felt deeply inadequate when faced with her intricate understanding of brain pathology and the ease with which she flitted from complex task to complex task. I, too, possessed a wealth of highly specialized knowledge, but none of it was applicable to caring for adult patients. The TICU was an alien environment to me, just as I'm sure my unit would have been to her. Indeed, I had once been asked to cross-train a pediatric nurse to take low-acuity neonatal patients, and she had been so disturbed by the minuscule size of the babies we cared for that after a few hours she clocked out for lunch and never came back.

When I returned from my afternoon break, Madeline was hanging up the phone. "Mr. J's family is coming in to take him off support," she said. "Can you help me set up?"

Planned withdrawals of care were also rare on my unit—that decision was usually made in the moment, and only after a series of increasingly aggressive interventions had failed. But in the case of Mr. J, we had plenty of time to prepare. His family had requested as little medical equipment as possible be present in the room, so we got to work removing the fall mats, sequential compression devices, and extra IV pumps before they arrived. Having spotted us rushing around, another nurse asked what was going on. Looking up from the pump she was wrestling with, Madeline said brightly: "We're going to give my patient the most beautiful death."

When the family arrived, I met them at the elevator and kept them company in the waiting room while the TICU staff removed Mr. J's breathing tube and disconnected him from the monitors. He died an hour later as the afternoon sun shone in through his windows, surrounded by his children and grandchildren, free of tubes and wires. It was the smoothest and most peaceful end of life I had ever seen—a far cry from the chaotic and anguished circumstances under which I was used to deaths occurring.

And although there were tears, it was indeed beautiful.

———————

We arrive at the second house and Alan stalks off, pulling the other stretcher behind him. I'm alone in the van with a corpse, and since he took the key with him, there's no AC. I also can't roll the windows down. As the temperature rises, I can't be sure if I'm starting to smell the body, or if it's just my imagination.

I watch it in the mirror. I can't help but feel like I'm intruding. A psychopomp doesn't usually bring spectators.

The silence is unbearable.

"Um, hi," I say, at a loss. "I'm RJ, and I'm pretty sure I'm not supposed to be here? I'm...I'm really sorry about that."

The body, predictably, does not answer. My hands are sweaty, and I wipe them on my dress, feeling foolish.

It feels like an eternity before Alan returns, sliding the second stretcher into place beside the first. "They're going to separate funeral homes, so it'll be another hour or two before we're done," he says as he starts the van and the AC mercifully starts to blow again.

"That's fine," I reply, although it wouldn't matter if it wasn't. We're two cities away from his apartment right now, and I have no way of getting back without him. He sets the GPS and starts driving.

Church Bells.

"The van is full, though?" I say incredulously, gesturing at the two bodies supine in the back, as he pulls over to read the text. "Don't we need to drop them off?"

"Yeah, but when it's a police call they have to send two of us. This one's going in Howard's van, not ours. We'll meet him there."

I've been in the van for four hours. My dinner was a few bites of salad and half a glass of sweet tea. The sun's going down, and I need to piss. I'm ready to scream.

"Okay," I say, and we merge onto the highway.

Quite a few nurses who wouldn't bat an eye at a gangrenous wound or rotting viscera are remarkably squeamish about corpses. Even the ones who are happy to do the aftercare—the last bath, taping the eyes closed, tying the hands with twill tape—balk at the idea of bringing the patient to the morgue afterward. I've never minded going, though. A room with a corpse in it is still just a room, and a person is no less worthy of dignity and respect after the life leaves their body. Alan felt strongly about providing that last kindness to those he transported, and although it's been over a decade since we split, that's something that stuck with me. I don't enjoy being the one whose patient is dying—I can't imagine many nurses do—but when there's a death elsewhere on the unit, I'm always willing to do the cleanup and bring the patient downstairs afterward.

"I don't know how you do it," a coworker once said as we sat chatting in our pod on a slow night shift, waiting for it to be time to start collecting labs. "It's spooky down there. It freaks me out."

I shrugged. "It really doesn't bother me. Now, if it was him"—I indicated my primary patient, for whom I had been caring every shift for the last eight months—"I'm not sure if I could bring myself to put him in the drawer."

"But," said another frequent morgue-goer, "if it *was* him, would you really want anyone else to do it?"

I chewed on that for a moment.

"No, I guess I wouldn't."

———

It's 11:00 p.m. and we're parked behind the medical examiner's office, waiting for someone to come unlock the door so Howard can drop off his passenger. It's taking a while, and my legs are cramping from being trapped in the van for so long, so I get out to stretch. I hadn't planned on being out so late, and my stupid sundress is proving woefully inadequate against the chill that's blowing in from the bay. Howard leans against his van and lights a cigarette, the smoke drifting in lazy clouds under the fluorescent glow of the loading dock lights. I'm considering bumming one off him, just for the hell of it.

Church Bells.

I wrap my arms around myself and shiver. Alan, more resigned than apologetic at this point, takes off his suit jacket and places it around my shoulders.

It's at this point that the medical examiner's staff finally arrive to take custody of the body in Howard's van, so I climb back into the passenger seat and wait while the two of them complete their paperwork and wheel the stretcher inside. My phone is at 5% power. I'm resigned to sleeping in the van tonight, probably with a corpse or two for company.

Alan comes back alone, and I buckle my seat belt. "Where to?"

"Home."

"I thought you had another call?"

"Howard felt bad for you." He laughs. "Want to get McDonalds?"

Yes. Yes I do.

———

My last shift at my first NICU was a Thanksgiving, and as I clocked in and went to check the assignment board, a bereaved family was walking out. After I finished getting report on my own patients, I went to check on the nurse whose baby had died. She and one of our techs had just finished the bath and were in the process of labeling the body bag and wrapping it in a swaddling blanket—a practice we commonly employed to disguise what it was.

"I'll take him down for you," I offered. "You can go home."

"Are you sure?"

"Yeah. I don't mind." I picked up the bundle and cradled it in my arms. Even through the layers of plastic and fabric, the baby was still warm. I sat with him in the rocking chair for a while, feeling the small heavy shape of him against my chest, closing my eyes and focusing on the quiet in that room—the darkness, the various equipment that would usually fill the space with beeps and hums now silent. I pressed a kiss to my fingertips and touched them to the sheet. When I was ready to leave, I called our unit secretary to stop traffic in the hallway so I could pass through discreetly.

One of the new hires approached me. "Can I come with you? I'm not really comfortable with all the death stuff, but I want to be."

I nodded, and she took my hand.

And together, we carried him to the end.

DELIQUESCENCE

Kelsea Yu

IT IS COLD where the dreamer lies. She is the only one of her kind in this dark, murky cage, but she is not alone. Claws tap out rhythms on her skull; fins brush patterns on her ribs. Slimy bodies drag themselves over her, under her, through her, while tender polyps sprout in the cavities that flesh and muscle once filled. Always, the water moves, its gentle undulations caressing her still form. Down here, the dreamer is but one of many oddities; creatures that call this place home, even if they should not.

Her eyes and ears are long gone, plucked clean by hungry things. Now, it is her bones that read the shape of the lake's combined whispers.

They tell her of the soft, beautiful boy, skin unmarred, eyes blue and whole.

They ask if she wants help staying hidden.

They warn her, and—

she does not listen.

————————

Clumps of wispy algae and clouds of swirling sediment tell her he is near. Unlike the thin, elegant tails of the lake's trout and char, his caudal fins are long and disruptive, giving him the water-feel of a much larger creature.

She is not afraid. She might once have been; a memory tries to surface, but it has sat unplayed for too long. She does not push her recall.

Curiosity fills her marrow. What remains of her body buzzes with electric desire to know why he is here, to know him, to be known by him.

He does not see her, and she cannot lift her hand to wave. Instead, she begs the lake for help. The lake does not like this, but it loves her.

A pumpkinseed sunfish swims by the boy. In the sunlit water, its orange-spotted scales shine golden. He follows it down, down to the dreamer.

He catches a glimpse of her. He reaches out to brush aside pondweed leaves, uncovering the shape of her skull. For a long moment, he stares. His shock is palpable, reverberating through the water between them.

Long after he's gone, she feels the weight of it, stirring something within.

He comes again and again, bringing new equipment. Staying longer, growing bolder. Soon, he is pulling up plants that have grown through her spine, clearing away piles of sediment crusted over her left femur and hips. His gentle caution as he frees her from the rocky floor, with chisels and brushes, stirs her to wakefulness.

He cannot seem to speak through his strange, translucent mask, but she does not need words. When he reaches out to place his hand on hers, she understands. His thoughts are a blunt force hitting her nape.

She knows him.

She *knows.*

And she remembers.

She loved a man. She made things easy for him; never told a soul. Telling would have ended them, and she would have done anything to stay his forever.

It was her body that did the telling. She knew she should kill the growing thing they'd made together, the evidence of their secret love. But when it came time, she found she could not bear to do it.

And so, he did it for—to—the both of them.

You're the girl who went missing on Grandaddy's farm, aren't you. You're Xinli.

The shape of her name is wrong in his thoughts, lifeless with each syllable's absent inflection. It reminds her of her missing pieces.

It is overwhelming, the tidal wave of everything. She has no eyelids to close, no ears to cover. All she has is the ceaseless feel of water picking away at her bones, and the touch of this boy's hand on hers. An echo of his grandaddy.

A promise.

He will take you away from us, the lake worries.

She does not care.

His grandaddy is dead, but he has inherited guilt. He will bury you in a wooden box and we will be parted forever.

She feels nothing.

Stay with us.

She loves the lake, but she loved her lover more. She loves him still, and he is gone. She should be angry at him, wary of his kin, but her bones hold only sadness.

She is attuned to the boy now, their stories connected long before he was born. His grandaddy put her and her soft, growing thing in the lake, and the boy will take her out. He returns to the lake, determined; she feels the moment he enters its strange waters.

She does not think she will mind leaving. She would like to rest within the earth, to be alone in her grief.

But she thinks of the soft, growing thing. Its bones were brittle when she joined the lake, carrying it tucked beneath her ribcage. Every piece of its body is long gone, dissolved into the murk or carried away by the current.

To leave is to leave it behind.

He swims down, down, and unfurls a net, slides it beneath her bones. Gently, he lifts, and her arms move for the first time since she sank to the depths.

She remembers the feel of it, the joy of it. Remembers the how.

Her arms wrap around his neck and pull him close.

He struggles, and she feels his terror. He does not understand, but she will help him understand. The lake listens. Tendrils of watermilfoil wrap around his mask, pulling it free. He gasps, and she embraces him, her hair filling his open mouth.

As he shakes, she brushes his cheek with her bony fingertips, as tender with him as he was with her.

You will live again, she whispers in the language of the lake as his lungs fill with water. *In a century, we will be home to coral and crabs, our sockets refuge to families of eels.* She paints him as beautiful a picture as she can imagine. *Someday, we will be one. Flesh picked clean; bones fused together by barnacles.*

One last string of bubbles escapes his lips before finally, he settles, and she curls around him.

You will love it here, she promises, and together they lie entwined.

ASK A NECROMANCER: FUN WITH FORMALDEHYDE

Amanda Downum

"THE WORST THING in here is the formaldehyde, right?"

That's what I asked my embalming instructor the first day we went into the lab, after our OSHA training and lectures on PPE. I'd had no funeral experience of my own before then and was carrying preconceptions that I'd picked up from pop-culture morticians, namely that a dead body was nothing to be afraid of and traditional formalin embalming was pointless and harmful.

To be clear, a dead body in and of itself *is* nothing to be afraid of, even a smelly one. We've moved beyond the miasma theory of medicine. *Dead* is not the problem; it's the pathogens that may still be alive. OSHA teaches the idea of universal precautions: i.e., treat all biological material as if it might be infectious. Morticians are rarely privy to a person's entire medical profile, and we don't assume that family members are either. I've worked with people who felt that wearing gloves when picking up a decedent at a house call was disrespectful to the family. I counter that unwittingly picking up a nasty pathogen and transferring it to the next house you visit is far more disrespectful. I'm not especially squeamish about corpses, but COVID immediately cured me of any inclination to skimp on PPE when interacting with the living.

But formaldehyde! It's a carcinogen! It's a dangerous chemical and therefore bad!

It is a carcinogen! It is toxic! Please don't drink it. But the false dichotomy of "chemical" (and therefore bad) vs. "natural" (and therefore good) is especially frustrating in our current climate of science ignorance and denial. Lava, fire ants, and hippopotamuses are all natural. So, in fact, is formaldehyde.

Formaldehyde is one of many aldehydes—from the Latin *alcohol dehydrogenatum,* or dehydrogenated alcohol—a diverse group of organic compounds. Traces of aldehydes such as cinnamaldehyde, vanillin, and trans-2-decenal contribute to the distinctive odors of cinnamon, vanilla, and cilantro.

Plants and animals produce endogenous formaldehyde, and it exists throughout the universe, including in interstellar medium. If a metal band hasn't written a song about that, one should. Recent research suggests that formaldehyde is a likely source of organic carbon solids in the solar system, which may have helped create the organic compounds and molecules that led to life on Earth. You're welcome?

On Earth, formaldehyde is an intermediate product in methane combustion, present in cigarette smoke, car exhaust, or forest fires. In humans, it forms in the metabolism of certain amino acids and is then further metabolized into formic acid. Formaldehyde breaks down quickly when exposed to sunlight or soil bacteria, and does not bioaccumulate. Which is good news for ghouls, maggots, and whatever cats may nibble on me after I die.

Russian chemist Alexander Butlerov first synthesized formaldehyde in 1859, but misidentified it. It was conclusively identified in 1867 by German chemist August Wilhelm von Hoffman. In mortuary school, these are the only two names we learn—from there it skips directly to formaldehyde's use in funeral embalming.

Phase 1: Discover formaldehyde

Phase 2: ?

Phase 3: Profit!

I couldn't teach that without derailing the lecture with my own questions, so I crawled down a rabbit hole. As it happens, when formaldehyde was first discovered, germ theory was gaining traction, to the lamentation of bacteria and the great rejoicing of hospital patients. Joseph Lister began using carbolic acid, aka phenol (also an embalming chemical), as an antiseptic in 1865. By 1889 the French chemist Auguste Trillat secured a patent to produce formaldehyde as an industrial reagent; Trillat in turn licensed companies in France and Germany for its manufacture. One of the first possibilities seen in formaldehyde was its potential use as a disinfectant.

This brings us to 1892, when a German physician and researcher named Ferdinand Blum was hired to test formalin (formaldehyde in liquid suspension) as a bactericide. While doing so, Blum spilled some on his fingers and noticed how the tissue hardened. This tidbit immediately caught my interest, for I too have had formalin leak through punctured gloves and noticed that exact same reaction. (Don't worry—it wears off.) Blum proceeded to test the fluid on tissue samples, and discovered that formalin preserved tissues as well as alcohol did, and with less distortion. And that, dear readers, is how it eventually became a staple in anatomical preservation and funeral embalming. In the United States, it replaced arsenic as a preservative—and no matter how much you may dislike formaldehyde, I assure you that arsenic is worse.

But wait! I have more formaldehyde-adjacent history to share. Ferdinand Blum was Jewish (though he converted to Protestantism after marrying his Catholic wife), and fled Nazi Germany in 1939 to continue his medical and scientific career in Switzerland. Blum's daughters, Pauline Jack and Gertrud Roesler-Ehrhardt, stayed in Germany to help Jewish refugees escape the Nazis. Pauline was an opera singer, through which circles she met the English sisters Ida and Louise Cook, who worked to smuggle the valuables of Jewish refugees across the German border so they could safely immigrate to Britain. (Ida Cook is also known as Mills & Boon romance author Mary Burchell.)

I set out to fill in the gaps about formaldehyde's history and discovered a Nazi-fighting opera singer. The world is an amazing place sometimes.

Fiction
PLUS ONE
Olufunmilayo Makinde

THERE WAS a time when the forest of horror was feared and left alone, when the spirits had to travel far to find people to torment, and even then they had to gather their strength and bide their time. They could weave dreams and cook up stories, subtle and overt temptations to bring people into their territory. At that time, people knew of the forest and its inhabitants, they called it an evil place, and to speak of the spirits within was taboo. Because they knew about it, they had rituals and spells to protect them. The spirits knew this, so they had to prepare for every incursion. Otherwise, they were powerless outside their forest and the world was safe from them, but that was a long time ago. It was before the missionaries came with their beliefs and unbelief and cut down the trees. Before the Mamry girls' school was built.

The school was built on a sliver of land, leaving the rest of the forest to encircle it in a half-moon shape. The only clear path out of the school was its front gate and the crumbling tarred road that led to it.

When you clear a house, the former occupants have to find new accommodation, and that was the case with the forest spirits. Some spirits were bloodthirsty and the chaos they wreaked upon the human world just as bloody, while some were more insidious. The tree spirits saw themselves as neither, but humans would call them evil all the same. They were beautiful beings who loved each other as family, but they hated people for tearing down their homes and for not being exactly like them. But they were also irrepressibly curious about people and their world; they wanted to be born and live with people. Like rats, they wanted to have a taste and leave the rest, not caring if what was left behind would be spoiled because of their bite. So they entered a pact to always come back to each other, and then they scattered themselves around the world, riding on the winds.

There is a bird that puts its eggs in another bird's nest and pushes out the other bird's real eggs. These tree spirits are just like those birds. Some called them Abiku, others called them Ogbanje, and the rest told their pregnant women to fix a small iron pin on their wrappers right on their bellies to ward them off and prayed to never have to call them anything.

The Abiku were born into this world but did not have a lasting wish to stay in it. The curiosity that drew them to become people would not last long enough to carry them past the age of seventeen. They were all beautiful children, they were born beautiful, they stayed beautiful, and they died beautiful. Then when they died, they did it all again like a faulty music player stuck on repeat. People hated Abiku for the anguish they brought them, as some of the spirits would pick a family and stick to it, going as far as to be born into the family and die young more than three times. People hated Abiku for the hope they brought with their birth and extinguished by leaving so decisively. They hated Abiku for the mounds of grave dirt they left in their backyards and the dread they now felt whenever they or their wives were pregnant. Those families hated Abiku because, after a while, they began to associate the smell of newborns with the stench of grave dirt and the fear of the inevitable. Far from their first home, the Abiku could only kill themselves when it was time to go, but it was different closer to home. It was different in the forest near Mamry girls' school, their source of power.

Mamry girls knew what the spirits were really called, but there is power in a name and they didn't want anything to have power over them. No one knows how this knowledge came to be, but every Mamry student passed it on to the new students, part of a twisted compilation of rules the students had made up to survive. They knew that calling the spirits Abiku or Ogbanje so close to their source of power would place a tag on them, like a mark on their soul, and the spirits would sink their teeth in, cling to it and never let go. So they called them "plus one," and even at that, they only called them this name in hushed tones. The students called them this because in Mamry, a plus one never went alone when it was time to go. The girls in Mamry lived constantly on the edge. Part of it was a side effect from being in a boarding school, with the many rules that seemed to hover over them like a fog. The rest of it came from the feeling that hung around, a feeling of constant fear and hopelessness.

New students try to fight it; they go back home after their first term and they cry. They cry rivers of tears in their homes and tell their parents tales of how twisted the school was and how evil spirits were everywhere. The lucky ones who were born to kind parents would be pulled out and transferred to a new school.

However, most parents who put their children in boarding schools wanted their children disciplined by someone else. The parents drawn to Mamry loved the school because it was the oldest school in the state, and that held some prestige. Another thing they loved was that the students who came out of that school were usually high achievers. Their results were usually higher than those of other schools whenever they met in competitions or before external examining bodies. This meant that for most of the students, complaining about Mamry would be met with a swift put-down by their parents. Finally, the students would return to school, keep their heads down, and try to follow all the rules to keep them off the radar of the spirits.

You can trust only yourself in Mamry, because the girl next to you, the one who shows you her answer sheet when you are writing your social studies tests, the same girl you switch food with on Monday mornings because she doesn't like akara and you don't like ogi, the girl you call your best friend, she could come up to you one day, ask you to walk her to the bathroom, and it would be the start of a terrifying new life.

To be in a boarding school is to embrace loneliness and the knowledge that no matter how homesick you get, your parents will not bring you back home. But whenever Mamry girls encounter a plus one, this knowledge is thrown away. With an aching desperation, you call home. You tell them that something is wrong in school and you need to come home. You tell them you are desperate. You are hitting all the checks the school management told your parents to watch out for in lazy students who cannot take the routine of boarding school. Your parents do not believe you.

Mamry girls tell stories, not for entertainment but to educate themselves. They know that they cannot rely on their teachers or parents. They can only rely on their own knowledge and hope that it will save them if they ever encounter a spirit.

The stories are always the same. When a plus one is being called home, their chosen companion hears the sound of drums. You, the chosen companion, hear the drums everywhere. You hear it in class, you hear it during study hour, and when you look around, it is clear that the beat only plays for you. The ba-dum-pums of the drum start out far, and if you're brave enough in your hostel after lights out, you take a peek out the window and you can barely see through the nets nailed around the window frame to keep flies out. You see a fire blazing far off at the foot of the old Iroko tree, but you don't go out to check. Once you focus on the tree, your vision becomes impossibly clear. You can see all the details without even leaving your room. The Iroko tree has a faint hollow at the base of its trunk; the hollow looks like it reaches deep into the tree and straight into the soil. You stare at the hollow, you cannot look away, the hollow seems to grow larger the longer you gaze upon it, and it looks darker than the night itself. The flames brighten and dim steadily as if to the rhythm of the drums you alone can hear. It is hypnotic, it is exciting, and for the first time that night, you realize that it is unusual. The unusual is never a good sign in Mamry, so you pull yourself away and go back to your bed. You can't sleep though, the drums are getting closer, you go back to the window to check but the fire hasn't moved and neither has the tree.

But the drums get closer still, and closer until they are no longer outside but right beside you, and then they're in your head too, rising and rising to an impossible crescendo. Then, as suddenly as they started, they're gone, and all you can do is stare at the reflection in the window and wonder why you don't remember getting out of bed.

The girl you can see in the glass is a familiar person with a strange look. You look wild, with a feverish look in your eyes and scattered hair you didn't notice get free of the rubber band you had put it in before. A strange thought pops into your head, and it remains with you even as you step away from the window. You think that you don't look like you belong in a house of stone, glass, and iron. You yearn for freedom but do not know what exactly it is. But as you fall asleep you remember that the wooden windows were open, and there aren't any glass windows around it, just the net. You don't know it, but your best friend stays awake and watches you until you fall asleep again. She has a smile on her face as her slender fingers reach out to your bunk and trace a pattern on it.

The next day you're distracted, you wake up confused and you feel strange, your school uniform makes your skin itch, it feels too rough, too artificial, and you have to leave your watch in the hostel because it gave you a rash. The classrooms are too loud and stifling, they reek of people and it's disgusting, as if everyone douses their bodies in chemicals every morning. You feel stifled, caged in, like a bird raised in captivity, longing for freedom, longing to be outside and away from people.

You are worried, so you call home again. Your parents have a choice again. They do not believe you. The sound of the drums echoes in your head as you battle with this knowledge.

You fight it at first. You want to go home. You want to be safe. So you dial your parents again under the watchful eyes of the hostel matron. Their answer does not change. This time, the shock you feel is muted, insulated by the sound of the drums. There is something wrong, but you are too far gone to do more than notice it.

———

That night, you hear the drums again, and this time you follow the sound, you see them around the fire then, the beautiful children. You know that this isn't good, but you can't bring yourself to care, they're all so beautiful, with their clothes made of leaves that look so soft, not like your polyester fabric nightgown. Their clothes look and feel right, and so does their company. The dancing spirits welcome you with open arms, and soon you are wearing a top and skirt made out of big soft banana leaves. You are slightly alarmed, but you spot your best friend dancing and it sets your mind at ease. If she is there, everything is okay. You dance and dance, and your best friend is there too, so it's okay. They dance near the Iroko tree and get closer to the hollow. They enter the tree through a doorway that forms when one of the dancers puts her hand into the hollow. The doorway seems to extend deep into the soil, and something in the darkness within sings beautifully. The ethereal voice wraps itself around you, it feels like silk on your skin. You are at a crossroads, but you don't know it yet. The light of the flames dances across their beautiful faces and yours too. A hand emerges from within the tree and beckons you in. You are so untethered from the world that a light breeze could blow you straight into the hollow of the tree.

You love your parents and have fond memories of them. But boarding school is a cocoon and it keeps those memories out, it traps the good feelings outside and leaves you to stew in the bad ones. All you have left is this choice. You hesitate briefly, but the sound of a dial tone echoes in your memory. You have made up your mind. You follow, and your best friend is there too, so it's okay.

Your body is found in the forest the next morning, you die in your sleep, a peaceful way to go, they tell your parents. Your parents are confused, but the autopsy shows no signs of foul play. So they mourn, and eventually, when their pain dulls, they accept that it was just your time. Maybe they mourn longer, for life even. You will not be affected by this if and when you see it. Their emotions are like cake in a display case to you; you can see it, but you can't touch it, so you are unaffected. Mamry girls know better than to tell adults anything, but they know, they don't talk about it but they know that plus one has taken another.

The drums usually start slow, so faint that you can almost believe that you're hearing your own heartbeat, ba-dum-pum it starts before dying down for a second. Then you hear it again.

You find yourself in the forest. Now you are one of the things that live in it. When the drums play, you are with your friend from school. Now you are one of the beautiful dancers beside, around, and inside the trees. Now you wait your turn to be born again and enjoy the world before returning to the trees. And if your new parents send you to Mamry, you will not return to the trees alone.

Fiction

MILES TO GO BEFORE I SLEEP

Beth Goder

CW: Mental health, suicidal ideation, death of a loved one

1.

The third time Zoey meets Death, she is unarmed except for a bag of twenty-seven kazoos.

2.

Zoey shouldn't be walking in the woods in winter, not when the ground is frozen, the wind pushing against her face like the bright prick of a needle. Pine trees huddle, hushed, under snow. Snow everywhere, reflecting a broken kaleido-scope sun.

As Death sweeps toward her, the woods fall silent, as if Death has caught up all sound. Their face is a blur, their arms and legs like the impression of limbs, like an afterimage burned across an eyelid. As always, Death's age never settles, or perhaps Death manages to be all ages at once.

Zoey clutches the bag of kazoos. She didn't expect to meet Death today. Not like this, with the chill of snow cutting into her ankles, with a satchel full of Entomology 201 test papers that she needs to grade, with the reek of cinnamon still cling-ing to her clothes.

Death holds out a hand, as if inviting her to join them. They ask if she finds the woods lovely, dark and deep, quoting her grandmother's favorite poem. Their voice is only an im-pression in her mind, like the memory of someone speaking.

She fumbles in the bag, pulling out a green kazoo with the picture of a beetle etched in the plastic. She doesn't know the rules of this engagement, this strange meeting, only that she will not lie down in the snow and freeze.

She places the kazoo in Death's hand, where it melts, green overflowing onto white snow.

3.

The first time Zoey met Death, she was falling from the red maple behind her grandparents' house, which she'd climbed to retrieve her bumblebee kazoo.

Her grandparents' house was in the Upper Peninsula of Michigan. "It's so far north," she'd tell her friends, sticking out her hand like a miniature Michigan map and pointing to her fingers.

She'd found the bumblebee kazoo folded into one of Grandma's huge tomes of poetry. The plastic had a bee etched on the side and stripes all along the body, with a circular membrane that looked like a stinger. She loved how the kazoo could change her voice into something it was not, an amplified buzzing, like laughter.

When her brother lobbed the kazoo into the huge red maple, Zoey shimmied up the tree without looking down. At the top, she stretched out, the tips of her fingers touching the kazoo. The motion of grabbing the kazoo was like the unbalancing of a board on a fulcrum.

For a moment, she hovered in the air. Death appeared, floating indistinctly in the sunlight. Zoey twisted her body as she fell, looking up at Death, whose body kept morphing.

She fractured her left wrist, broke her leg, and bruised a rib, but she did not die.

The kazoo was cracked down the side. Although Grandma glued it back together, it never made quite the same sound.

Whenever Zoey was near the red maple, she felt like she couldn't breathe, her heart a drum.

She'd felt that way about other things, too. She didn't know how to name the beast that sat on her chest. She didn't know what to call her anxiety.

4.

When Zoey was a child, she could not stand to be around chemicals. An intense anxiety would overtake her body whenever her mother used bleach, whenever the exterminator sprayed around the house, whenever bread turned moldy.

But no one else seemed to mind. As a child, she could not put into words her sense of urgency, the sense of falling away, falling forever.

As she got older, it only got worse.

5.

In the woods, Zoey reaches into the bag of kazoos.

A magical flute would be more appropriate. There's a precedent. A flute carries a certain dignified weight.

Instead, Zoey has kazoos: one black as night, one shaped like a star, seven with insects etched on the sides, one filled with rain, one gossamer kazoo that's hardly there at all, and many others besides. Twenty-seven kazoos.

This is what the universe has given her to face Death. A paper bag, sitting on a stump, filled with kazoos. Isn't that just what life is like? Unpredictable and unfair and so uncannily ridiculous?

Death waits, inclining their blurred head, absently working time between their fingers like a silk scarf.

The insects that normally rustle in the woods have disappeared. Zoey has done research on so many of them—wasps, coccinellids, cicadas. Their absence frightens her more than anything else.

Death's mouth never moves, but the words echo in Zoey's head. These are the rules. She is getting another chance to live, which is more than most people, but it is not because she is special. She is another human, and like all humans, full of desires and flaws and contradictions.

But she has seen Death twice before, that blurred phantom, and so there will be a game.

Twenty-seven kazoos rustle in her hands, marked with their meanings. If she can choose the correct one, she'll be able to leave.

She has three tries to get it right.

The woods keep silent, like the space between breaths. Trees uproot themselves and rumble over, roots scraping across the snow. They enclose Zoey and Death, stopping the wind, but somehow, it grows colder.

"Choose," says Death, with a voice that is not a voice.

6.

Reasons Zoey is in the woods:

Professor Tupper sat in his ratty orange armchair, looking uncomfortable. His office smelled like cinnamon from the cookies he always baked for Christmas, miniature circles bathed in spice. "I have some bad news," he said.

No tenure means no stability, no more teaching Entomology 201 with hikes through fields in the chill of morning, no more coffee by the library with her boyfriend, no more walks in the woods, not after she moves, as she has had to do for work again and again.

Escape. She is the queen of stupid decisions. It was easier to walk into the woods than to call her boyfriend, who she knows will not move with her. Easier to dip into the trees than to begin the cycle of application after application.

Whenever she finds mold, or bleach, or fertilizer, she feels her chest tighten so hard that she thinks she's dying. She cannot stand to be anywhere chemicals have been. In her mind, she can't stop thinking that anyone, everyone, could have walked through pesticide. She starts avoiding everything that feels dangerous, which means never taking the path by her house, which means not inviting her friends over (with their shoes that have stepped in mysteries), which means her life shrinks in just a little bit tighter, until it squeezes the breath from her. She doesn't understand why she is this way and other people aren't.

The woods are lovely, dark and deep.

7.

The second time Zoey saw Death, she was sixteen. Grandma was in the garden digging up potatoes for stew.

The house in the Upper Peninsula was set away from the rest of the world. A refuge from gossip and homework and other high school troubles. In the morning, Grandma had made her oatmeal with goat's milk and read to her from a collection of poetry about autumn. Each poem fell softly, like a leaf. Two of the pages stuck together. Careful not to tear the paper, Grandma pried the pages apart with the antique letter opener she kept on the mantel. In the middle, she found the bumblebee kazoo.

In the garden, Death hovered above Grandma. Zoey searched for the trowel, anything to fight off Death, but she'd left the trowel down by the turnips. What use would it have been? Zoey pulled the kazoo from her pocket and hurled it at Death. Like a buzzing bee, the kazoo embedded itself in Death's head, in the folds of their ear.

Death enveloped Grandma until she blurred. Grandma dropped her basket, raining potatoes everywhere.

They were miles from the nearest hospital, and the old pickup truck couldn't go over fifty.

It didn't matter. There was nothing anyone could have done.

8.

In the woods, in the prison of trees, Zoey rummages through the kazoo bag. She is running out of time. If she doesn't act, she will freeze, here in the woods, in the darkness that is creeping toward her.

She selects a kazoo as bright as the sun. It warms her hands. Light spills from between her fingers, until her cage of branches grows impossibly bright.

Light overwhelms her. She cannot find the mouthpiece of the kazoo, so instead of blowing through it, she flings the kazoo at the space where Death stands.

Death laughs, a persistent buzzing. Or perhaps it is a sob. She once took a research trip to Canada to see the metallic green buzzing beetles, and Death sounds like this, like a swarm of beetles circling her head.

Through the glow, Zoey can see the outline of Death's form. Death's hand closes over the kazoo, extinguishing it like a candle. The kazoo drops to the snow—a cold, dead star.

She's fallen into a fallacy of opposites. Death is not darkness, not the other side of light. Death is something much more complex.

In the bottom of the bag, a kazoo shifts, hiding itself. It is the absence of space. It is nothingness. She wants to touch it, but it scares her.

"Two more choices," says Death.

9.

Anxiety has been with Zoey for as long as she can remember. Anxiety is the airtight chamber, the heart squeezed too tight, fire's fervid heat.

It is the mind-killer, the wave, the ellipsis.

Anxiety is her own mind folded in on itself, endless, forever, forever.

She doesn't understand why her thoughts get stuck, why she has an intense fear of chemicals, why she is becoming afraid to even leave her house.

It is years before she is diagnosed with OCD.

10.

At Grandma's funeral, Aunt Silvia stopped to straighten Zoey's hat, as if Zoey cared about how she looked.

"Your grandmother was quite a woman. Got her pilot's license at twenty-two." Aunt Silvia pulled a pin out of her own hair and stuck it in Zoey's.

One of Grandma's poetry anthologies was tucked in Zoey's bag. Grandma never kept a diary, but she took notes in the margins of her poetry books, dated by entry, creating a patchwork of her life.

"She lived a full life," said Aunt Silvia, as if that mattered at all, as if that made Grandma any less gone.

11.

The woods are growing darker, tree branches curled over her like laced hands.

Death waits for her second choice.

She runs her hands through the bag of kazoos, choosing one that is universe-dark. It is a rich, deep ebony, an inkwell bleeding with unwritten words. It is the opposite of nothingness, full and dense.

Zoey opens her hands, letting the jet-black poison of the kazoo spill out.

Death absorbs it all, for they have seen millennia. They contain each life, each breath, every possible sorrow, every moment of discovery.

In the bottom of the bag, the kazoo that embodies absence waits. It calls out to her with its nothing voice.

In a voice that is not a voice, Death tells her she has one choice left.

12.

This is how Zoey experiences OCD:

The thought.

Again and again.

Again again again.

The thought, overwhelming her.

The thought. Again again.

The waterfall crashing over her.

Again again again again.

It is falling into forever.

It is the loop that becomes an infinity symbol.

13.

Zoey rummages through the bag of kazoos. Colorful hard plastics fly through her hands like cards in a magician's deck. One kazoo keeps slipping away, into the corners of the bag. Its outlines are unclear. All its physical attributes fade—color, size, shape—but she knows, with the certainty that comes when one's life is draining away, that it's what she's looking for.

The kazoo made of nothingness.

Death stretches up, until she cannot tell their arms from the branches. A cool wind rushes through.

No, Death is saying, over and over again, in a voice like the wind.

The nothingness kazoo brushes against her fingers.

Zoey upends the bag of kazoos, laying them out stark on the snow. Whenever her hand nears the nothingness kazoo, Death motions, and the wind sweeps it out of her grasp.

What does she care for the rules of this game, when Death has already broken the most important one? It was supposed to be her choice.

She picks out one kazoo after another.

The rough, green kazoo branches out like a tree, a seed grown from the soil of her hands. Death points, and the tree withers.

Next, three black kazoos fly like birds. Death swallows them, like a magician vanishing a coin.

The paper kazoo is as soft as a sigh. As she holds it, words flow, telling the story that is her life until this moment.

"The woods are lovely, dark and deep," says Death. It is like an incantation. The paper burns until the kazoo is ash.

The kazoo blue as twilight makes a space of light around them, then drifts up to the sky to outline the stars.

She's used three choices and more, but none of them matter.

Zoey faces Death, her heart beating wild. "I'll use them all until I find it."

"Not yet," says Death, in that voice which is everywhere and nowhere all at once.

14.

During her worst moments, her thoughts go:

It is everywhere it is in the house it is in on my hands I can't I can't I'm going to die please it's in my hair I can't breathe let me let me please I need it to stop I need it to stop I need it to I can't breathe it's everywhere it's on my clothes please let me please I can't I can't stop

why can't I stop?

15.

Zoey's greatest secret is this: she does not fear death.

Death is only an absence, an unmaking.

How many times has she longed for that great blanket of nothingness to fall over her, like new snow?

16.

Is it possible to grieve one's own life? Zoey has wasted so much time ruminating. So much time trapped by her OCD.

Her grief is a shallow bowl, spilling over. A long path into twilight.

Is there a way forward after so much suffering? She asks herself this again and again, and still cannot find an answer.

17.

Zoey grabs the nothingness kazoo, cupping her hands over it.

It is the last choice she has to make.

The kazoo yawns wide. Instead of throwing this kazoo at Death, she sticks a finger in, then her whole hand, and then she is tumbling down and through. The world becomes filtered and silent. A grey tide pulls at her.

She knows this isn't what she wants, but it feels like the only choice she has left.

Zoey waits, her breath still, and it feels to her like she is not alive or dead. It feels to her like she is nothing at all.

She thinks of her life as a path that's narrowed, a twisting stairway she has always been walking down. She remembers her grandmother telling her that the things that feel inevitable are not always so, that gentle moments have power.

She sees her life as an ocean, beating like an inverted heart. Everything that's happened to her is only one more wave crashing against the shore. This vastness swallows her, and she pushes back, because if she stays here she will never see the snow again, the lovely, dark woods. Maybe the desire to feel the coldness on her skin again is enough.

She thrusts her hand out of the opening of the kazoo, pushing her fingers into the snow. Her hope is a fragile thing, an uncertain thing.

Death grabs her hand. Their touch feels like one million beetles crawling.

Limb by limb, Zoey is pulled back. Death folds their hands over the hole in the world, then subsumes the nothingness kazoo.

Color returns to the hollow, even though it is only the white of snow and branches leached of pigment in the twilight.

The remaining kazoos melt into the snow, a rainbow of colors.

Death fades, and Zoey is left only with her breath.

In her hand, she is clutching the bumblebee kazoo.

18.

In her research, Zoey becomes fascinated with the Pharaoh cicada. *Magicicada septendecim* spend most of their lives dormant in the ground, emerging to see the sun after seventeen years of waiting.

Maybe it is possible to be buried for so long, only to emerge, to rise up, ready to live.

19.

Zoey starts a type of therapy called Exposure and Response Prevention (ERP), in which she must face her greatest fears. All her life, she has avoided chemicals, but now she sprays herself with insect repellent and cleans with bleach. She carries moldy food around her house, spreading spores. For her, it is like drowning, her brain convincing her with each breath that she is going to die.

But she doesn't die. Instead, slowly, her world opens up.

Zoey goes outside more often. She invites her friends over, not even checking their shoes for toxins when they come into the house. She spends less time lost in her particular fears.

ERP doesn't erase her worries, her repetitive thoughts. It simply creates a space around the fear, and in this gap, she is able to make a choice.

She keeps the bumblebee kazoo in her satchel. Every day, she cleans it with bleach, despite her fear of chemicals. Every day she touches the bleach-covered kazoo and feels the fear well up inside of her.

Zoey develops a different relationship to anxiety. Instead of running from anxiety, she runs towards it. It isn't easy. Some days are worse than others. Sometimes she imagines her thoughts as a waterfall, rushing past her but not touching her.

Zoey embraces uncertainty as much as she can.

20.

Zoey will always have a complicated relationship with Death. Once in a while, she sees Death in the most unlikely places—at the grocery store by the bananas; in the shape of a cloud; at the back of her lectures, really paying attention.

Each time, she thinks to herself, "I have miles to go before I sleep."

In summer, she watches the cicadas, their lacy wings stretching for the first time, and she marvels at how they emerge ready to live their glorious lifespans, with all of their uncertainty, with all of their freedom.

Poetry

SÉANCE

Elizabeth Wing

In the employee housing lobby
where we stamp our feet and drink weak coffee
the toaster oven catches on fire

flames leaping from its maw like curses
so and we yeet it out into the snow.

When they ask *who forgot to clean it,* we say *all of us.*
It sizzles against the snowbank, one wisp of smoke straining up.

My boots are heavy but I'm floating.
In the early morning coyotes wake me
their voices almost human. Who is guilty? *All of us*
But no one wants a Cassandra.

ghosts only dustbunnies at the back of the cabinet.
ghosts only crumbs in the bottom of the oven. Ghosts
        growing restless,
asking: *why have we been ignored?*

At fifteen you threw plums at a boy's car, whipped donuts in a
        parking lot.
Two years later we raised his voice from the dead in a circle of
        salt, a book fell
open and we sprinkled
round agates looking for his words.

Coyote pelt across the fence: *pests.*
we disagreed.

The dead bear gifts and no instructions on how to open: cigar
    box. hibiscus bud
spiraled tight.
an apple from the bank of the mercury pond, which everyone says
will give us terrible dreams.

You biked the white-knuckle curves
of the California highway to his shrine. Prayer flags tugged
    in the wind.
Found a deer skull, which you balanced
on the handlebars, all the way home.

I read somewhere that this year there were for the first time
fewer movies where someone says *let's get out of here*
than movies where someone says *stay*.

After the fire we will loot the ghost houses for stories.
We will go through the places burned down to concrete rectangles
and pull out a bottle of ink, rubber chicken, stray barrette.
But that's another story. That's the easy story.

So much to do we say.

Coyotes say *No*. Coyotes pause crossing the road for one lantern-
    yellow stare. They
have always been so close.

What I'm telling you here is
the toaster oven sizzles in the snow, when we pull it out it leaves
an imprint of soot, and all of us say *so much to undo*.

Fiction

LITTLE TRINKETS

A. J. Sharpe

WHAT *are you doing here?*

You lie alone in a field, discarded—they do not need you anymore.

You stare sightlessly at the bright blue sky, pale clouds drifting lazily across it like soft boats on a calm sea. The sun shines down, golden rays licking at your cold, unfeeling skin. The long grasses around your body sway gently in the breeze, their quiet whispers left unheard.

What are you doing here?

The magpie lands on the ground beside you, feathers gleaming blue-green in the sun. It cocks its head as it gazes at you, its beady black eyes staring at your stillness.

What is that?

It flutters next to your head, attention captured by the jewel dangling from your ear.

As shiny as a hazelnut!

It pecks at you, sharp beak snipping into your lobe and dragging the prize from it before swooping away, the precious stone dangling from its mouth.

Thank you!

What are you doing here?

The starling chirps, ruffling its soft speckled feathers as it lands in the hedgerow. It inspects you from afar, waiting for a sudden movement that never comes.

What is that?

Hopping down, its pointed yellow beak begins to pluck at your scalp, collecting strands of your deep brown locks.

As fine as horsehair!

Done with its harvest, the starling flies from your body and disappears back to its home, its beak full of strands for the nest.

Thank you!

What are you doing here?

The crow caws as it dives down and lands beside you. It tucks its glossy black feathers tight to its body as it inquisitively hops upon your corpse.

What is that?

It buries its sharp black beak into your eye socket, ripping the eyeball from it.

As blue as a cornflower!

It swallows your eye, savouring the taste as it begins to pick at the rest of you, devouring your flesh.

Thank you!

Poetry

QUIETUDE II

Adamu Yahuza Abdullahi

in the market square
where the bandits opened fire
you took one of the grenades
into safety
in your mouth
& you outran your legs
you got home
trembling
your mother
asked what happened
but you chewed on silence
because your mouth is a slaughterhouse
and everything it touches
becomes the lamb.

ONE MORE EPISODE

Ashok Banker

I STILL REMEMBER the first time Soleil came down to watch TV with my mother. It was three months after the world started ending, though we didn't know it was ending then. Just thought it was another bad year in a string of bad years, like how people used to say every decade was the hottest on record until they stopped keeping records altogether.

Mom had been dead for twenty-six years by then, but that didn't stop her from showing up one autumn evening, materializing on our old brown corduroy couch with a Virginia Slim between her fingers and a gin and tonic sweating on the coffee table. She looked exactly as she had in '97, down to the oversized cream sweater she'd bought at Macy's during their Christmas sale and the slight smudge of coral lipstick at the corner of her mouth that she'd never quite mastered fixing.

I stood in the doorway of my apartment, keys still dangling from my hand, grocery bags forgotten at my feet as a half-gallon of milk slowly warmed to room temperature. The TV clicked on by itself, the screen warming up with that old cathode tube glow, even though I hadn't owned a tube TV since college.

"Shh," Mom said, though I hadn't spoken. "It's starting."

The familiar bass line of the *Seinfeld* theme filled the room. I remained frozen, wondering if the stress had finally broken my mind, when there was a flash of golden light that made my retinas spark and dance. Suddenly, there was someone—something—sitting next to my long-dead mother on my couch.

It took me a moment to understand what I was seeing. The sun. Not the burning sphere from the sky—though looking out the window, I could see it was indeed missing from its usual place, leaving the evening oddly dim and colorless—but a woman made of gentle light, her edges soft and shifting like a candle flame. She wore what looked like a vintage nineties power suit, but made of condensed sunbeams, and her hair moved like solar flares in zero gravity.

"Hope you don't mind me dropping in," she said, her voice carrying the warmth of a perfect spring morning. "I'm Soleil." She kicked off her shoes (strappy sandals that seemed to be made of dawn light) and tucked her feet under herself. The couch cushion compressed beneath her as if she had actual weight and mass, though I could see the fabric of the couch through her slightly translucent form.

Mom offered her the cigarette pack with the casual familiarity of old friends, but Soleil declined with a graceful wave of her luminous hand. "I don't smoke," she said. "Bad for the complexion. Gives me sunspots!" Her laughter was like summer afternoon heat rippling off asphalt, and where her feet had been, I noticed the carpet had begun to fade slightly as if from years of sun exposure.

"Your mother's told me so much about you," Soleil said, turning to face me. Her eyes were like twin eclipses—bright rings of fire around perfect darkness. "I hope you don't mind me joining your little viewing party. It gets lonely up there sometimes, especially these days." She gestured vaguely at the window, where the empty sky was turning an unsettling shade of green.

I meant to say something rational, something like "You can't be here" or "This isn't possible" or even "Would either of you like some milk before it goes bad?" Instead, what came out was: "You watch *Seinfeld?*"

"Oh, honey," Mom said, taking a long drag of her cigarette. The smoke curled up toward the ceiling in impossible spirals, forming tiny gray question marks that hung in the air like punctuation marks in search of sentences. "Everyone watches *Seinfeld.*"

"Even stars?" I managed to ask.

"Especially stars," Soleil replied. "You think it's a coincidence they called it 'Must-See TV'? We literally had to see it. Cosmic law." She winked at me, and for a brief moment, my apartment was filled with the kind of light you usually only see in desert summers.

That's how it started. They became regular viewing partners after that, meeting every evening at 7:30 sharp for reruns. Soleil never missed an episode, except during autumn when she'd sometimes sleep in or call out sick.

"Seasonal depression," Mom explained with a knowing look, though I wasn't sure if stars could get depressed. "Even the sun needs a mental health day sometimes," she added, and Soleil had nodded gratefully, her light dimming to a soft autumn sunset glow.

Living with a celestial body takes some adjustment. The first week, all my houseplants grew wild, stretching their leaves toward Soleil whenever she sat on the couch. The spider plant that had barely survived my erratic watering schedule sprouted dozens of babies, sending green tendrils cascading down the bookshelf. My sad grocery store orchid burst into ridiculous bloom, its flowers an impossible shade of purple I'd never seen before.

"Sorry about that," Soleil said, noticing me stare at the jungle my living room was becoming. "I can try to tone it down." She dimmed herself slightly, though the plants still swayed toward her like sunflowers tracking the sky.

"Don't you dare," Mom said, tapping a fresh cigarette out of her pack. "This place could use some life." She had opinions about my decorating choices, or lack thereof. "Remember our old house? All those window boxes your father built?"

I did remember. Mom had grown geraniums and marigolds, bright splashes of color against the white siding. After she died, Dad had let them wither. I'd helped him pull out the rotted boxes the following spring, neither of us mentioning the real reason they needed to go.

Soleil and Mom quickly developed their own viewing rhythm. Mom always sat on the left side of the couch, Soleil on the right. They had favorite episodes—Mom loved anything with George's parents, while Soleil had a soft spot for Kramer's entrepreneurial schemes. "Reminds me of Mercury," she said once. "Always cooking up some wild plan or another. You should see what he's been up to lately." She paused. "Actually, maybe better if you don't."

They developed in-jokes I didn't quite understand, references to episodes mixed with what I assumed were cosmic events I'd never heard of. Sometimes they'd finish each other's sentences or burst out laughing at the same moment, even before the punchline landed.

"It's about timing," Soleil explained when I asked. "Your mother gets it. Comedy, orbital mechanics—it's all about timing."

I learned to make three cups of tea every evening, though I had to buy special heat-resistant cups for Soleil after she melted through two of my regular mugs. "Earl Grey for your mother, chamomile for me," she'd say. "I'm trying to cut back on caffeine. Did you know there's a nebula in Carina that's basically pure coffee? Keeps the whole spiral arm up at night."

The apartment developed strange quirks. The shadows never fell quite right when Soleil was there, and sometimes small objects would orbit slowly around her head when she got particularly excited about a scene. The wall behind her favorite spot on the couch began to show signs of subtle radiation damage, the paint taking on a peculiar iridescent quality that reminded me of soap bubbles.

Mom's cigarette smoke continued to form impossible shapes—not just question marks now, but entire scenes from whatever episode they were watching, miniature gray versions of Jerry's apartment or Monk's Café hanging in the air like memorial sketches. They never dissipated completely; I'd find them later, tucked into corners or hiding behind picture frames, little pieces of preserved laughter.

One evening, during the episode where Jerry's girlfriend looks either stunning or hideous depending on the lighting, I caught Mom watching Soleil instead of the TV. There was something soft in her expression, something I remembered from long ago.

"You remind me of someone," she said during a commercial break. "Someone I used to know. Same kind of…brightness."

Soleil's light flickered briefly, like a candle catching a breeze. "Your son's father?"

Mom nodded. "He had that quality. Like he was lit from within." She took a long drag of her cigarette, the smoke forming a delicate spiral galaxy above her head. "After I left—after I died, I mean—I used to worry about him. About both of them. Sitting in the dark."

I wanted to tell her we'd been fine, that we'd learned to navigate the darkness, but the words stuck in my throat. Besides, we all knew it wasn't entirely true.

"Well," Soleil said, her voice as warm as noon, "good thing I'm here now." She reached over and patted Mom's hand. Where they touched, Mom's form became briefly translucent, suffused with golden light, and for a moment I could see through both of them to the worn fabric of the couch beyond.

The next episode started playing, and they turned their attention back to the screen. But something had shifted, settled. The room felt warmer, and not just because of Soleil's presence.

Willow joined them about a week later. She'd been gone four years by then, my oversized basset hound who'd never quite fit the breed standard but had captured every heart she encountered. The American Kennel Club might have sniffed at her excessive height—she'd stood well above their precious thirty-two-inch limit at the withers—but she'd been pure basset where it counted: in the droopy eyes, the velvet ears, and most importantly, the soul.

She didn't fade in gradually like Mom had, or arrive in a flash of light like Soleil. One moment the couch held just my two regular viewing companions, and the next Willow was there, padding across the room as if she'd just been out for one of her leisurely neighborhood patrols. Her silky brown fur caught Soleil's light and transformed it into a halo, making her look like a stained glass window's interpretation of a dog.

"Well, hello there," Soleil said as Willow approached the couch. My heart caught in my throat—Willow had always been nervous around strangers in life, especially unusual ones, and I couldn't imagine anyone more unusual than an anthropomorphized star.

I needn't have worried. Willow gave Soleil a single sniff, apparently decided that a celestial body was nothing to be concerned about, and heaved herself up onto the couch between them. She turned around three times (her signature move, perfected over years of couch-napping), flopped down with her head on Soleil's lap, and promptly began to snore.

"Oh, my," Soleil said, looking delighted as little puffs of steam rose where Willow's drool evaporated against her luminous form. The steam clouds drifted upward, forming tiny cumulus formations near the ceiling that occasionally sprinkled warm drops back down, thankfully missing the couch. "She's perfect."

Mom reached over to scratch behind Willow's ears, her incorporeal fingers somehow managing to find that sweet spot that always made Willow's back leg twitch. "She's a proper basset hound," she declared, with the same tone she'd used to defend my career choices to judgmental relatives. "Never mind what those show dog people say."

"What do they say?" Soleil asked, genuinely curious.

"Oh, something about her being too tall." Mom waved her cigarette dismissively. "Bunch of nonsense. Look at those eyes. Look at those ears. She's as basset as they come."

As if to prove Mom's point, Willow let out a snore that would have done any basset proud, followed by a sleep-woof that made both Mom and Soleil jump, then giggle like schoolgirls.

"What's she dreaming about?" Soleil wondered, as Willow's legs began to twitch.

"Bears," I said automatically, remembering how she used to wake herself up barking at dream-bears, then look around confused when she couldn't find them. "She always dreams about bears."

"Bears?" Soleil's light flickered with amusement. "Why bears?"

"Well," Mom said, settling back into the couch, "there was this one time at the park…"

And so Willow joined our nightly routine. She added her own rhythm to our viewing sessions—snoring through the cold opens, waking up for any scene with food (especially if it involved Jerry's kitchen), and occasionally sleep-woofing at crucial plot points. Her dream-bears became more elaborate, perhaps influenced by Soleil's presence. Sometimes now, tiny ursine constellations would appear in the steam clouds above her head, acting out whatever ursine adventures she was experiencing in her sleep.

She also proved to be an excellent mediator on the rare occasions when Mom and Soleil disagreed about episodes. It's hard to maintain an argument about whether "The Contest" or "The Soup Nazi" is the better episode when you have a snoring basset hound draped across both your laps, occasionally kicking in her sleep as she chases imaginary bears through her dreamscape.

"She's getting bear drool on my photons," Soleil complained once, but she was grinning as she said it, her light pulsing with barely contained affection.

"Some of my best particles," Mom agreed solemnly, before they both dissolved into laughter that made the windows rattle slightly.

The only time Willow ever showed any sign of distress was when the sounds from outside would grow particularly loud—the wailing sirens, the distant explosions, the strange humming that sometimes made the air itself vibrate. Then she would whimper softly in her sleep, and Soleil would shine a little brighter, creating a bubble of warm light that seemed to push the darkness and noise back, just a little bit further, just a little bit longer.

I first noticed the world was really ending one Tuesday evening during "The Chinese Restaurant." Mom was explaining to Soleil why waiting for a table was such a quintessentially human experience ("Stars probably don't have to wait for anything, do they, honey?") when I glanced out the window and saw that the moon had turned green.

Not a subtle sage or a gentle mint, but the violent green of copper oxidation, of nuclear warning signs, of things that really shouldn't be that color. It hung in the sky like a broken traffic light, casting sickly shadows across the city.

"Ah," Soleil said, following my gaze. "I was wondering when you'd notice that." She shifted uncomfortably, causing Willow to grumble in her sleep. "Luna's been having a rough time lately. We all have, up there."

"Is that why you started coming down?" I asked.

She was quiet for a moment, her light dimming to the soft glow of a winter afternoon. "Partly. It's…complicated. The kind of complicated that doesn't translate well into any earthly language." She gestured vaguely at the ceiling. "Things are changing. The old laws—orbital mechanics, gravitational constants, the really fundamental stuff—they're getting wobbly. Like a top that's running out of spin."

"Is there anything that can be done?" The question felt inadequate even as I asked it.

"Oh, honey," Mom said, in the same tone she'd used when I'd asked her if the doctors could make her better. She took a long drag of her cigarette, the smoke forming a double helix that slowly unraveled into chaos.

Outside, the sirens had become a constant background noise, like crickets in summer. The city's emergency alert system had been cycling through the same messages for weeks: Stay indoors. Avoid looking directly at the moon. Report any unusual geometric shapes appearing in your home. If you hear singing from the walls, do not attempt to harmonize.

During commercial breaks, I'd sometimes go up to the roof of my apartment building. The city looked different every time—buildings that had been there for decades would vanish overnight, replaced by structures that seemed to follow non-Euclidean architectural principles. The downtown skyline had developed a habit of rearranging itself when no one was looking, like a child's blocks being shuffled by an unseen hand.

Time started behaving strangely too. Episodes that should have been thirty minutes would sometimes last for hours, or pass in what felt like seconds. Once, we watched the same scene of George explaining his "jerk store" comeback for what seemed like days, the dialogue looping and fragmenting until the words lost all meaning. None of us mentioned it afterward.

More and more often, I'd catch Soleil staring out the window with an expression that made my chest hurt. Her light would flicker and dim, like a candle struggling against the wind. During these moments, Mom would reach over Willow and take Soleil's hand, and for a brief instant, their combined glow would push back the darkness that seemed to be seeping in through the walls.

The plants in my apartment continued to grow, but now they produced flowers in colors I had no names for, their petals arranging themselves into impossible fractals. The spider plant babies began to orbit their mother plant like tiny green moons. My rescued orchid developed a consciousness and started humming show tunes.

"Jerry would love this," Mom said one evening, as we watched a group of people outside trying to catch what looked like geometric shapes that had escaped from a mathematics textbook. "It's like that time he dated the woman who looked different in every lighting. Remember that episode, Soleil?"

"That was months ago," I said.

"Was it?" Mom frowned. "Time is so strange now. Even stranger than it was when I was…away." She never used the word "dead," as if speaking it might break whatever spell allowed her to be here.

"Time was always strange," Soleil said softly. "You humans just noticed it less when it behaved itself. Like gravity. Or bears," she added, as Willow let out a particularly emphatic sleep-woof.

The TV itself had started showing signs of temporal distortion. Sometimes the laugh track would play before the jokes, or we'd catch glimpses of episodes that hadn't been filmed yet—couldn't have been filmed yet, with the original actors now decades older. Once, we saw an episode where Jerry was played by a shifting cubist sculpture, while Kramer had become a sequence of prime numbers in human form.

"Don't worry about it," Soleil said when she noticed me staring. "Reality's just getting a bit…experimental these days. Think of it as a director trying some new things with an established format."

But I caught the worried glance she exchanged with Mom, and the way they both looked down at Willow, still peacefully sleeping between them, blissfully unaware that the laws of physics were unraveling around her dreams of bears.

Despite everything—the green moon, the geometric shapes eating downtown, the way time had become more suggestion than law—we kept to our schedule. Every evening at 7:30, or what the clocks claimed was 7:30, we'd gather on the couch. Mom would light her cigarette (she'd been smoking the same pack for months now, never running out), Soleil would kick off her light-spun shoes, and Willow would claim her spot between them.

I developed my own rituals. Three cups of tea, carefully prepared: Earl Grey for Mom in her old ceramic mug with the chip on the handle, chamomile in the special heat-resistant quantum cup for Soleil (ordered from a website that only existed on Thursdays), and an empty bowl near Willow that somehow always ended up full of dream-bear drool by the end of each episode.

"You know what I miss about being alive?" Mom asked one evening, during an episode where Jerry's girlfriend couldn't believe he'd never seen *Schindler's List*. "Food. Real food. Not that I don't appreciate the tea, honey," she added quickly, taking a sip from her eternally full cup. "But I miss the taste of things. Remember those Sunday breakfasts we used to make?"

"Blueberry pancakes," I said. "And that turkey bacon Dad always burned."

"He claimed he liked it extra crispy," Mom laughed, her cigarette smoke forming tiny dancing pancakes that floated up to join the constellation of bear-shapes near the ceiling.

"I miss different things," Soleil mused. "Supernovas. The dance of solar flares. The way planets feel when they spin past." She paused. "Though I have to admit, these episodes are better than most celestial entertainment. Mercury tries to organize game nights, but it's mostly charades, and you try playing charades with gas giants. Jupiter always cheats."

"How does Jupiter cheat at charades?" I asked.

"Extra moons," Mom and Soleil said in unison, then burst out laughing.

The world outside continued its descent into chaos. The laws of physics became more like physics suggestions. Gravity started taking weekends off. Color escaped the visible spectrum and had to be herded back by teams of specialized scientists. Time began flowing in multiple directions at once, leading to awkward encounters between people's past and future selves at grocery stores.

But in our apartment, we had our constants. The familiar bass line of the theme song. Kramer's entrance. George's latest scheme. Elaine's shove. Jerry's raised eyebrow. The laugh track that somehow kept playing even after the studio audience had evolved into pure energy and ascended to a higher plane of existence.

We developed in-jokes about the apocalypse. When the episode about Jerry's "evil twin" played, Mom pointed out that most people now had at least three quantum superpositioned versions of themselves walking around. During "The Soup Nazi," Soleil mentioned that his soup was nothing compared to the liquid singularities being served at the new café down the street—"Talk about no soup for you. One sip and you literally cease to exist!"

Willow slept through most of it, occasionally twitching or woofing at her dream-bears, which had evolved along with everything else. Sometimes now they wore suits and carried briefcases, conducting important bear business in her dreams. Other times they merged into a single ur-bear, a platonic ideal of bearness that even Soleil found impressive.

"That's some quality immortal archetype work there," she said admiringly one evening, as a particularly elaborate bear constellation performed a waltz above Willow's sleeping form. "Most humans have to study for years to manifest something that stable."

"She's always been an overachiever," Mom said proudly, reaching down to scratch Willow's ears. "Remember when she learned to open the fridge?"

"That was less impressive and more expensive," I reminded her, thinking of all the lunch meat I'd had to replace.

"Details," Mom waved her hand dismissively. "The point is, she had initiative."

The TV followed its own increasingly abstract rules. Characters began switching roles mid-scene. Props gained sentience and went on strike. Once, every laugh track was replaced by the sound of distant waves breaking on shores that no longer existed. Through it all, we kept watching, kept commenting, kept finding things to laugh about.

Even as the walls of my apartment began to occasionally phase out of existence, revealing glimpses of other dimensions where history had taken different turns, we maintained our little bubble of normalcy. When multicolored rain started falling upward past my windows, we just pulled the curtains and turned up the volume. When time loops caused the same scene to repeat seventeen times, we treated it like a recap episode.

But I couldn't help noticing that Soleil's light was growing dimmer, requiring more and more effort to maintain her human-like form. Sometimes, during particularly chaotic moments outside, she would flicker like a candle in a storm, her edges blurring into pure energy before she pulled herself back together. Mom would pretend not to notice, but I caught her watching Soleil with the same expression she'd worn in her final days at the hospital—a mixture of concern, love, and helpless frustration at forces beyond her control.

The end began during "The Finale." Fitting, I suppose, though it wasn't the actual series finale we were watching—just a regular episode that happened to be about endings. The green moon had split into three pieces, each one rotating in a different dimension. The city outside had mostly transformed into a series of abstract mathematical concepts connected by streets made of pure probability.

Soleil was having trouble maintaining her coherent form. Her light flickered and pulsed, sometimes bright enough to cast multiple shadows from the same object, sometimes so dim I could barely see her outline on the couch. Mom's cigarette smoke had stopped forming shapes and just hung in the air like frozen tears.

"You know we can't stay much longer," Mom said during a commercial break that kept cycling through advertisements for products that had never existed. Her voice was soft, but it carried the weight of inevitability. "Things are…shifting. Even here."

She was right. The walls of our sanctuary were beginning to blur at the edges. The TV signal increasingly picked up broadcasts from parallel universes where *Seinfeld* was a tragedy about the heat death of the universe, or a documentary about sentient soup, or just nine seasons of silent cosmic horror.

"I know," Soleil said. Her voice sounded distant, like starlight reaching Earth long after its source had died. "The fundamental forces are unraveling faster than we expected. I need to go back up, try to hold things together as long as I can. Though between you and me"—she leaned forward conspiratorially, trailing stardust across the couch—"I think the universe is ready for a rerun."

Willow snorted in her sleep, perhaps sensing the tension in the room. In her dreams, the bears had gathered for what looked like a formal goodbye party, wearing top hats and carrying tiny ursine briefcases.

"One more episode?" I asked, my voice cracking slightly. It was what I'd said to Mom that last night in the hospital, though then it had been about reading one more chapter of the book we'd been sharing.

Mom and Soleil exchanged looks. Outside, another piece of the moon crumbled into abstract expressionism.

"One more episode," Mom agreed, reaching for the remote. She had to try three times before her incorporeal hand could grasp it—the boundary between her existence and nonexistence was growing thin.

Soleil brightened briefly, mustering her remaining energy to cast a warm glow over our little group. Willow's tail thumped against the cushions, and her dream-bears raised tiny champagne glasses in a final toast.

The familiar theme music started playing, though now it seemed to contain harmonies from the beginning of time, bass lines from the birth of stars. I settled onto the floor at their feet, my own cup of tea warming my hands. The light from the TV mixed with Soleil's fading glow, creating patterns that reminded me of summer afternoons from my childhood, of Mom in her garden, of Willow chasing imaginary bears through the park, of all the small moments that make up a life.

"You know," Soleil said softly as Jerry delivered his opening monologue, "I've seen galaxies born and stars die. I've watched civilizations rise and fall on worlds you'll never know existed. But this"—she gestured at our little group, at Mom's eternal cigarette, at Willow's peaceful sleep, at the familiar scenes playing out on the TV—"this has been something special."

"It really has," Mom said, and for a moment her form solidified completely, looking exactly as she had that last good day before everything changed. She reached out and took my hand, and I could almost feel her touch.

The episode played on as reality continued to dissolve around us. The laugh track began to include the sounds of distant nebulae and the music of spinning pulsars. Kramer's entrance sent ripples through multiple dimensions. The studio audience had become a quantum superposition of every possible reaction to every possible joke.

We watched it all together, this family we'd somehow become—the dead mother, the living son, the star who had chosen to spend her evenings watching sitcom reruns, and the oversized basset hound who dreamed of bears. Outside, the world was ending, but in here, for one last half-hour that might have been an eternity, we were exactly where we needed to be.

The world could wait until after the credits rolled.

And until then, well, we could always find time for one more episode.

AUTHOR BIOS

ARDA MORI (she/her) is a Malaysian writer of the darkly fantastical. Her work is forthcoming/has been published in *All Worlds Wayfarer, Horns & Rattles Press, Apparition Lit, Fifth Wheel Press,* and elsewhere. Find her on Bluesky at @armori.bsky.social or at ardamori.wordpress.com.

AMANDA CECELIA LANG is a horror author and aspiring femme fatale from Colorado. Her stories haunt the dark corners of many popular podcasts, magazines, and anthologies, including *Gamut, Ghoulish Tales, Cast of Wonders, Uncharted,* and Flame Tree's *Darkness Beckons.* Her short story collections *Saturday Fright at the Movies: 13 Tales from the Multiplex* and *The Library of Broken Girls* are now available. You can stalk her work at amandacecelialang.com—just don't be surprised if she leaps out at you from the shadows.

MICHAEL HESSEL-MIAL (he/him) teaches writing at the University of Minnesota. His speculative poetry draws on world poetry traditions and histories of social struggle. Similar work can be found at *Urban Pigs, State of Matter,* and forthcoming from *Katabatic Circus.* Michael's older digital poetry work has also appeared in *Columbia Journal, The Fanzine,* and *Queen Mob's Tea House.* Michael is Jewish and a father. He believes in unions, prison abolition, and a free Palestine. He's writing a science fiction epic poem called *Song of the Participants.* You can find him by the handle @mrpoemguy on Substack and Bluesky.

DANIEL OLUREMI is a fourth-year Nigerian medical student. He has forthcoming fiction and poetry works in *Nightmare* and *Apex* magazines. He is also the first runner-up of the DKA Short Story Writing Competition 2024. In his free time, he enjoys discussing books and series with his friends, and he hopes to get a dog one day.

RJ AURAND is a southern Appalachian writer, poet, and lover of the bizarre whose work has appeared in or is forthcoming from *Blanket Gravity Magazine*, *Small Wonders*, *Solstitia*, and *Tales & Feathers*. Connect on Bluesky @rjaurand.bsky.social or at rjaurand.com.

KELSEA YU is the Shirley Jackson Award–nominated author of *Bound Feet, It's Only a Game,* and *Demon Song.* She has over a dozen short stories and essays published or podcasted in magazines such as *Clarkesworld, Apex, Nightmare, PseudoPod,* and *Fantasy,* and in various anthologies. Find her on Instagram or Twitter as @anovelescape or visit her website kelseayu.com.

OLUFUNMILAYO MAKINDE is a Nigerian lawyer and writer who to her dismay seems to find herself doing more of the former than the latter. She is absolutely in love with the horror genre. This is her first published work of the genre, but you can find her other work in *Full House Literary* and *The Periwinkle Pelican.*

BETH GODER is an archivist and author. Over forty of her short stories have appeared in venues such as *Escape Pod, The Magazine of Fantasy and Science Fiction, Analog, Clarkesworld, Lightspeed, Flash Fiction Online,* and Horton's *The Year's Best Science Fiction & Fantasy.* You can find her online at bethgoder.com.

ELIZABETH WING is a writer based in Portland, Oregon. Wing's recent work has appeared in venues such as *Poetry Currency, The Washington Square Review, Witness Magazine,* and *Pic-*

tura Journal. She feels most alive catching garter snakes, playing the harmonica, and yelling into spaces that echo.

A. J. SHARPE, queer horror author and collector of dead things, has always enjoyed the morbid and the gross. Armed with an MA degree in Creative Writing from Aberystwyth University, Sharpe hopes to use her skills to horrify and nauseate. You can find out more about her and her writing at: ajsharpe.co.uk

ADAMU YAHUZA ABDULLAHI, THE PLOB, TPC V, is a poet and visual artist from Borgu, Nigeria. His debut poetry collection, *The Rainbow Is Not as Beautiful as My Ruins,* is forthcoming from Felis Catus Press.

ASHOK BANKER writes and lives in the liminal spaces. This is his first appearance in *The Deadlands.* His short fiction has appeared in *Asimov's, Lightspeed, Nightmare, Weird Tales,* and *Year's Best Fantasy,* among others, and has been nominated for the Bram Stoker Award, the CWA Award, and won the Utopiales Nantes Award for his horror and dark fiction.

STAFF BIOS

SEAN MARKEY publishes websites for a living and has always dreamed of starting a publishing company (about Death). He lives with his wife, Beth, and a handful of well-traveled pets, in northwest Spain.

E. CATHERINE TOBLER is a writer and editor. You might know her editing work from *Shimmer Magazine.* You might know her writing from *Clarkesworld, Lightspeed,* and *Apex Magazine.* A trebuchet and Oxford comma enthusiast, she enjoys gelato and beer in her free time. Leo sun, Taurus moon. You can find her on Bluesky @ecatherine.com.

NICASIO ANDRES REED is a writer, poet, and essayist whose work has appeared in venues such as *Shimmer, Fireside, Lightspeed,* and *Uncanny Magazine.* He's read slush for *Strange Horizons,* edited manuscripts for award-winning authors, and owns five different copies of *Moby Dick.* He lives with his family in Cavite province in the Philippines.

INKSHARK is a scandalously queer illustrator, author, and editor who lives in the rainy wilds of the Pacific Northwest. He enjoys exploring with his dogs, writing impossible things, and painting what he shouldn't. When his current meatshell begins to decay, he'd like science to put his brain into a giant killer octopus body with which he promises to be responsible and not even slightly shipwrecky. Pinky swear.

DAVID GILMORE is a writer, reader, and editor out of St. Louis, MO. His work has been featured in *The Rumpus* and at Lindenwood University, where he also received his MFA. He lives with his wife and son and spends his free time manning a stall in the Goblin Market selling directions to various Underworlds in exchange for rumors and information on where he can find his muse.

AMANDA DOWNUM is the author of *The Necromancer Chronicles, Dreams of Shreds & Tatters,* and the World Fantasy Award–nominated collection *Still So Strange.* Not content with armchair necromancy, she is also a licensed mortician. She lives in Austin, TX, with an invisible cat. You can summon her at a crossroads at midnight on the night of a new moon, or find her on Twitter as @stillsostrange.

LAURA BLACKWELL is a freelance copy editor and Shirley Jackson Award–winning writer. Her publications include stories in *Chiral Mad 5, Nightmare,* and the 2023 Shirley Jackson Award winner *Aseptic and Faintly Sadistic: An Anthology of Hysteria Fiction.* Visit her website—and if you like, sign up for her newsletter—at pronouncedlahra.com.

CHRISTINE M. SCOTT has been a professional graphic designer, website developer, and brand consultant for more than thirty years. She is the creative director and copublisher of Nosetouch Press and has coedited seven anthologies, including the folk horror anthology trilogy *The Fiends in the Furrows.* She is also an artist and craftsperson—several of her handcrafted items were included in *Game of Thrones: The Compendium,* printed by Chronicle Books for HBO. For a complete list of her pursuits, please visit christinemariescott.com.

FELICIA MARTÍNEZ is a writer and artist born and raised in Eastern New Mexico, though home is now the San Francisco Bay Area. She is a 2023 Dream Foundry Contest for Emerging Writers finalist, an honor she achieved with a beloved work of flash. Find her on Bluesky and Instagram as @feliciafm.

ANNIKA BARRANTI KLEIN is a freelance editor with a writing habit. Her work can be found at annikaobscura.com. She is supervised by a cat at all times.

www.ingramcontent.com/pod-product-compliance
Lightning Source LLC
Chambersburg PA
CBHW030011010826
48973CB00009B/2761